SANCTUARY TALES

SANCTUARY TALES

VOLUME ONE

The Sanctuary Series

Robert J. Crane

SANCTUARY TALES
VOLUME ONE

SAVAGES
A FAMILIAR FACE
Robert J. Crane
Copyright © 2012 Reikonos Press

THE LAST MOMENTS OF THE GEZHVET
THE GREENEST FIELDS
A PRINCESS OF SOVAR
THIEVING WAYS
Robert J. Crane
Copyright © 2013 Reikonos Press

All Rights Reserved.

1st Edition

AUTHOR'S NOTE
This book is a work of fiction. Names, characters, places and incidents are products of the author's imagination or are used fictitiously. Any resemblance to actual events or locales or persons, living or dead, is entirely coincidental.

The scanning, uploading and distribution of this book via the internet or any other means without the permission of the publisher is illegal and punishable by law. Please purchase only authorized electronic editions, and do not participate in or encourage electronic piracy of copyrighted materials. Your support of the author's rights is appreciated.

No part of this publication may be reproduced in whole or in part without the written permission of the publisher. For information regarding permission, please email cyrusdavidon@gmail.com

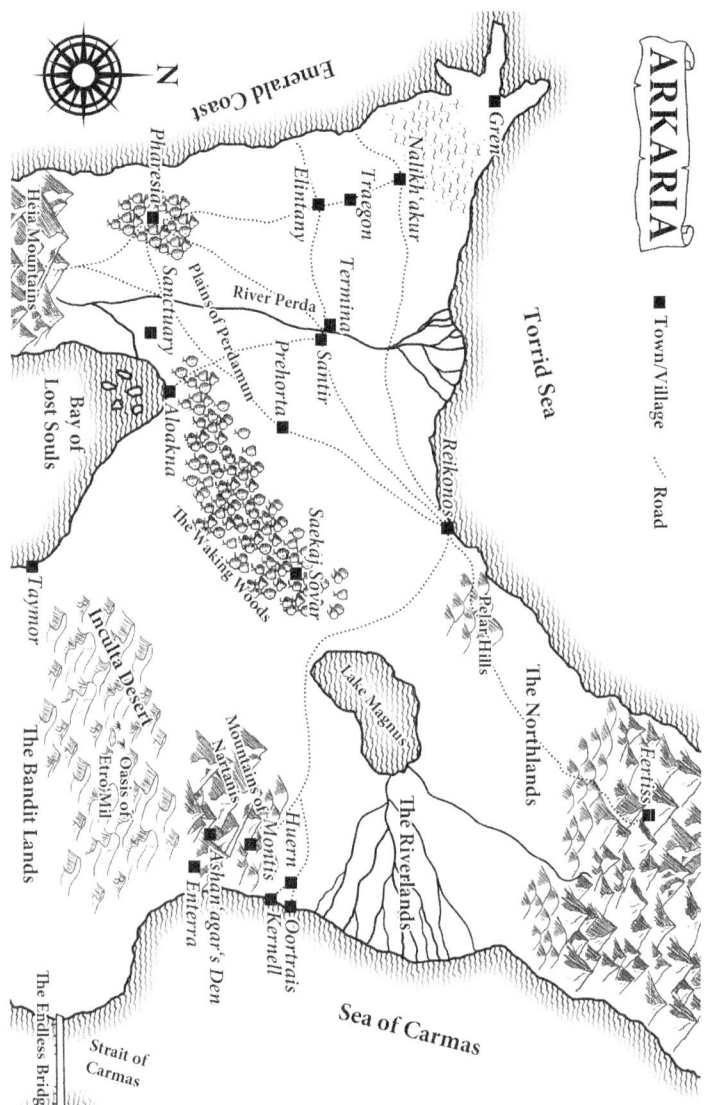

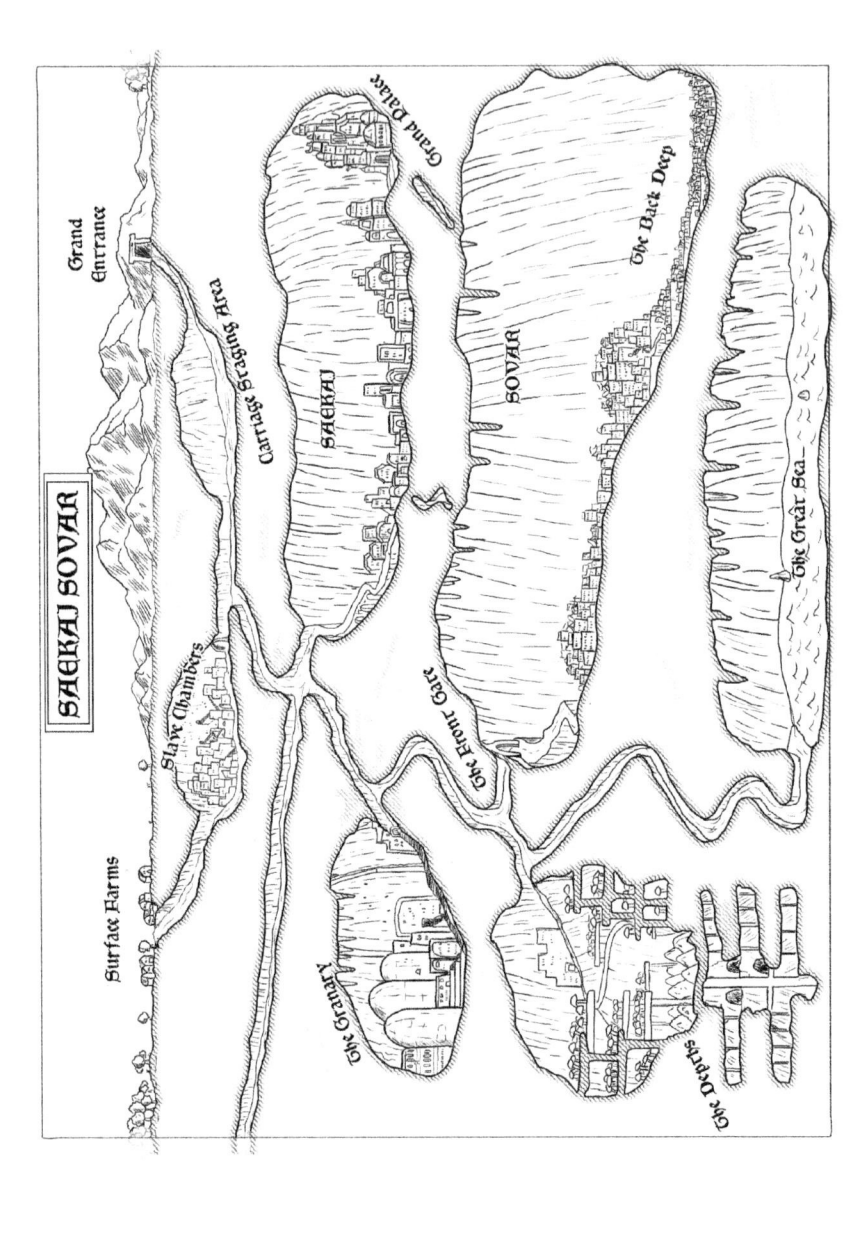

Acknowledgments

The stories collected in this book were written sporadically, over a greater than two year period. During that time, I received help from the following:

Heather Rodefer – dutifully beta-read every single one of them, provided feedback, and helped me avoid the most egregious errors.

Shannon Garza – beta read at least one of them, I think it was A Familiar Face.

My Dad – helped me with a specific passage of The Greenest Fields to help me get it right.

I should thank Edgar Rice Burroughs because I borrowed his titled "A Princess of Mars." Also, the first line was inspired by the awesome Andrew Stanton-adapted movie of a couple years ago. You should watch it if you get a chance.

And then come the usual suspects – Sarah Barbour on editing, Karri Klawiter for the cover and Nick Ambrose for formatting (and editing on A Familiar Face and Savages, actually). Muchas gracias, gang. I don't really know what I'd do without you. Flail about uselessly, I suspect.

Thanks of course as always to my mom and dad, wife and kids.

SAVAGES

Note: This story takes place during the events chronicled in **Defender: The Sanctuary Series, Volume One**, in the six month gap between chapters 15 and 16.

One

It had been almost three months since the Enterra expedition and Cyrus Davidon spent his days moping. For the last three weeks he had not left Sanctuary, and the walls of the guildhall were beginning to make him feel as if he were in a prison.

Mornings were the toughest part of his routine. His good friend and constant companion Andren usually didn't awaken until the afternoon, and spent the rest of his day parked in the lounge, drinking from the kegs of ale, broken by the occasional sip of Dark Elven brandy or Gnomish cognac. Cyrus had tried Pharesian whiskey with him, but afterwards regretted it for three days of punishing headaches.

This morning found Cyrus in the Great Hall, picking over eggs with gravy. It would normally have appealed to him, but food had lost its flavor. He habitually dined alone so when a tray found its way onto his table he looked up in surprise.

"Cyrus," came the voice of a gnome. "I've watched with great concern as you sink lower and I'm here to do something about it," came the squeaky voice of Brevis Venenum. Brevis was two feet tall and garbed in a black robe that would have fit on a doll. "I have a proposition for you."

"A proposition?" Brevis had not spoken to him since they had met – when Cyrus had accidentally stepped on the diminutive enchanter.

"Indeed." Brevis lowered his voice. "I've learned the location of a temple far from here, where zealots of a wealthy cult used to worship. I'm told they left quite a hoard of gold behind. I'm leading an expedition."

"Why would the cultists leave behind gold?" The question popped out before Cyrus could stay it.

"They were attacked while on a pilgrimage and never came back for it. But it works out well for us, doesn't it?"

"I suppose."

"I have a small group assembled. We leave tomorrow."

"I see."

"We'll split the treasure," Brevis continued. "It's good to have a first class warrior joining us; lets me sleep better and focus on the planning, knowing you'll have things well in hand."

"I didn't say I was in yet," Cyrus protested.

Brevis leaned across the table to give Cyrus a pat on the glove and nearly fell over. "We meet in the foyer tomorrow at daybreak. It will be several days' journey." With a quick salute, the gnome stepped off the bench and walked away.

"I didn't say I was in," Cyrus mumbled under his breath. He considered sitting around Sanctuary, wandering the halls aimlessly, and remembered advice Terian had given him – anything would be better than the nothing he was doing. "All right," he called at the retreating back of the gnome, "I'm in!"

Two

Cyrus waited in the foyer the next morning, before it seemed anyone else was awake. The sound of heavy footfalls on the stairs jarred him from his thoughts, and he looked to see the troll, Vaste, move into sight from under the spiral of the staircase. Cyrus tucked himself behind the fireplace; he did not care for trolls.

Vaste stood a head taller than Cyrus, yet shorter than most of his kind. His skin was a light green, almost glowing, with no hair to crown him and teeth that were barely concealed by his overlarge lips. He wore a black tunic, which was unusual for a healer. He also wore a sash that accompanied his class of spell caster and carried a staff that was tall enough to be used as a walking stick, with a gem at the top that pulsated white, glowing with energy.

The troll entered at a slow walk, pausing in the middle of the foyer. *Please don't see me,* Cyrus thought. Vaste turned, saw Cyrus, and gave him an informal nod. "How goes it this fine morning, Warrior Davidon?"

"It goes," Cyrus grunted.

"Indeed," Vaste said with a pleased smile. "I haven't seen much of you in the last few months. How are you coping?"

Now he's asking personal questions. Cyrus felt the heat rise in his face. "Fine."

"Perhaps it's the monosyllabic response, but I doubt it."

Take the hint and go away. Vaste continued to stare at him, polite smile on his face. Cyrus did not reply. *I don't want to talk with you, troll scum. Leave me alone.*

"You know," Vaste said, "I find that the best way to get through an awkward moment – and that's what we're having here, an awkward moment – is to find common interests. Me, I enjoy reading. You?"

Cyrus stared at him. "I…no, I don't read much."

"Hunting?" Vaste asked. "I don't have much interest in the killing of wild beasts myself, but often Sanctuary sends out hunting parties around the plains and into the woods – we are feeding a sizable number of people after all, and that requires fresh meat. Is that something you enjoy?"

"I...no," Cyrus replied, flustered.

"I'm sorry for assuming," Vaste replied. "I thought perhaps since you enjoyed battle, hunting might be a natural extension of that."

"In battle your quarry fights back," Cyrus said in annoyance. "And I'd have a hard time catching a deer in full plate mail, wouldn't I?"

The troll shrugged. "I've seen Vara do it, but I suppose she is more agile than yourself." The dark eyes of the troll focused on him. "So...what do you do to fill the long days?"

Cyrus clenched his teeth. "I...I..."

"Excellent!" came the squeak of Brevis's voice. "Punctuality is an attribute highly prized." He was flanked on either side by Gertan and Aina, his close companions. Aina, who was tanned, had her auburn hair pulled back in a knot and wore leather clothing that exposed more than would be desirable on most. Her face was impassive and rarely showed a hint of feeling. Gertan was a dark elven warrior with a sycophant's smile, nodding his head whenever Brevis spoke.

"I have to go," Cyrus said with an overly ingratiating smile directed at Vaste. He stepped forward to stand next to Brevis.

"Step close," Brevis said with a grin, "we're teleporting east of the Inculta Desert, to the very last portal in that territory. We'll need to be careful: there are no kingdoms or principalities; it's a land under the dark shadow of banditry."

Vaste took a few steps toward them, causing Cyrus to look at him. "We're leaving now; you might want to step back." When the troll smiled, Cyrus felt a small discomfort. "He's not coming along, is he?"

"Would you like to try healing yourself?" Vaste asked. "Because I'd guess that being mortally wounded thousands of miles from home would be an ill way to end your trip."

"He's one of the best healers in Sanctuary," Brevis said with uncontained glee. "He gets ten percent of the base profit, plus ten percent of the share of anyone he has to cast a healing spell on."

Vaste's toothy grin caught Cyrus's attention. "I anticipate you're going to make me wealthy."

"He also knows the resurrection spell. That may come in handy."

"You know, in case you die," Vaste interrupted. "A bargain at only twenty percent per casting."

Brevis, unperturbed, continued. "Aina, if you would?"

Aina was a druid, a spell caster with the ability to control nature as well as being blessed with the magics of teleporting from one place in Arkaria to another, tied to the giant stone portals that dotted the lands. Her hands swirled through the air as she murmured inaudible words under her breath. Her hair stirred from within its knot by a wind swirling around them in the foyer.

Cyrus's eyes met Vaste's and his look of incredulity was matched by the wide smile on the troll's. "This will be so much fun," Vaste said. "If we get into battle, your life is in my hands!"

A tornado's fury consumed them as the winds of Aina's teleportation spell swept them away.

Three

Cyrus felt the soft crunch of sand under his boots as the winds faded. Blue skies replaced the dingy torchlight bouncing off the stone walls, and a beach of white sand under his feet stretched to clear blue seas making their way up to the horizon. He glanced back to see the ovoid circle of rock that was the portal; magical objects somehow tied to teleport spells.

Gertan, Aina, Brevis and Vaste were scattered around him. The troll seemed to be taking enormous pleasure in the beach; he had taken off his boots and was mashing the sand between his green toes. "I was raised in the coastal swamps," he explained. "I heard of places like this, but since my people were defeated in the last war they don't leave the homeland much."

"Shame it's at all," Cyrus muttered under his breath.

"All right." Brevis commanded their attention. "We head south along this beach for two days; then head inland when we reach a road. We follow the road for three days, and it's through the jungle from there."

"No horses?" Cyrus asked.

Brevis shook his head. "We'd lose them in the jungle. And…" The gnome looked down. "My pony can't keep up with the rest of you."

"And you, on foot, will have better luck?" Vaste smiled down all seven feet of his frame to the two foot tall gnome. Brevis hissed an angry and inaudible reply and began stalking down the beach.

The first two days passed slowly. Gertan and Aina contributed little to the conversation; Aina, in fact, said nothing, and Gertan only nodded after every point Brevis made. The gnome dominated the conversation. Cyrus determined not to speak unless spoken to. Vaste also said little, leaving Brevis to fill the conversational gaps.

"I asked for Orion's help, did I tell you that?" Brevis said for tenth time that day. "He turned me down, said it was foolish to venture into these lands. We'll show him; I tell you, since the Enterra expedition he's lost all heart for adventure. Why, just the other day…" Brevis prattled on while Cyrus took advantage of his height to move ahead, taking long strides that would leave the gnome behind.

When he was far enough away to be out of earshot, Cyrus let out a deep sigh that was mirrored by one to his left. He looked toward the sound and felt a scowl part his lips. Vaste was only a few paces behind him. "I don't know about you, but I'm not sure I can take another week of his griping."

"It's not so bad."

Vaste's eyebrow cocked. "I apologize; I had marked you for someone with a great deal more sense."

Dark clouds drew over Cyrus's face. "You insult me, troll."

"At last," Vaste replied. "Did you assume that I'd allow your verbal jousts at me forever without an eventual riposte?"

"I have not…" Cyrus gritted his teeth, biting back the reply he'd planned. "I have tried to be as cordial to you as possible—"

"Then you're failing."

"I think it would be best," Cyrus said, commanding every ounce of patience he had left, "if we stuck to the task at hand and left any conversation for another time."

"Very fine," Vaste said, complexion turning to an even deeper green. "Since the day I first left my homeland, I've been exposed to a constant diet of people who hate trolls with every fiber of their being. Until now," he said, thick eyebrows furrowing, "I've never met anyone within Sanctuary so ignorant as to treat me this way without cause. I suppose I thought we had a higher standard for our members."

"You don't know the first thing about me," Cyrus snapped at him.

"Well, not to get philosophical with you, but likewise." Vaste's scowl deepened. "At least you're giving me reason to dislike you." The troll slackened his pace as Cyrus sped up, letting the warrior leave him behind.

Four

Cyrus walked ahead of the group for the rest of the day. When they made camp on the edge of the beach that night, he stayed away from the fire, preferring to sleep early and awaken before any of the others. By the light of dawn he wandered down the beach, heading south, until something caught his eye in the distance. He approached a little closer and realized it was a stone bridge; enormous columns stuck hundreds of feet out of the sea, supporting a causeway that extended beyond the horizon. When he returned to camp he made mention of it to Brevis, who waved him off.

"Yes, the Endless Bridge, seen it a thousand times. Impressive, yes? Extends off over the Strait of Carmas. Not really sure where it goes."

"But who built it?" Cyrus asked him. "And how? It's longer than any bridge I've ever seen."

"Amazing," Vaste commented. "I heard about it while I was studying in Fertiss. I'd heard rumors it leads to a different land."

"Irrelevant," Brevis said. "We have a mission. There's no time for exploration!"

"Have you heard of anyone crossing it?" Cyrus asked Vaste, curiosity overcoming his acrimony toward the troll.

"A few," the troll replied. "Can't say I've read any accounts of anyone who's come back." He smiled ruefully. "Take that for whatever it's worth."

"It's worth less than a heap of horse dung," Brevis interrupted. "Now, about the temple we're going to: there were accounts of their gold..."

They broke camp after a breakfast of fresh fish that Aina had caught the night before. They had camped at the entry to the road Brevis had mentioned, but it seemed more like a dirt path.

Cyrus once more led the way. Vaste walked close to the gnome, expression neutral. Every so often, Cyrus would catch a note of annoyance cross the troll's face, but all he heard was the occasional grunt from Vaste whenever Brevis reached a point in his utterings that seemed to require concordance.

After three days and nights of walking the path, the flat lands around the beach had turned into swamps, then rough plains until finally they came to an almost unbeaten divergence from the path that led into the jungle that had appeared around them over the last half day. "This is it!" Brevis declared with a squeak of triumph. "Only a couple more days and we'll be there, collect the treasures, and we can teleport home."

"Lovely," Vaste commented, swatting at a mosquito that looked larger than Brevis.

The path through the jungle was scarcely that. At times it became near impassable. Rocks, vines and other natural obstacles blocked their way. At one point Brevis was nearly swallowed in a pit of quicksand while arguing with Vaste about their heading. Cyrus sighed, not quite in relief when Gertan and Aina recovered the gnome from what could have been a tragic end.

At nightfall, they had seen no sign of a temple and Brevis ordered them to make camp, annoyance cutting through the facade of politeness the gnome had shown to this point. "Don't understand," he muttered, "it's supposed to *be* here." He had been rambling under his breath for most of the afternoon.

Their camp spot was in the middle of the "trail" in the increasingly impassable jungle. Surrounded on two sides by water, the small strip of land they sat upon did not offer much space for sleeping. Rain had begun at midday and was persisting even now; there was no wood available that had not been soaked. In spite of Aina's best efforts, they had no fire.

Cyrus sat with his back to a tree, out of conversational earshot of the rest of the group. Brevis was complaining, judging by the look on his face. Gertan was nodding along while Aina sat stonefaced, watching the gnome gesture in frustration with his hands pointed skyward.

"Isn't this fun?" came Vaste's voice from the darkness. The troll appeared next to his tree.

"No," Cyrus replied, returning his gaze to the gnome, who was now throwing a fit. "But," he added, "it could be worse."

Vaste looked at him. "What would be your definition of worse?"

Dark caves and claws, yellow eyes and green scaled skin flashed through Cyrus's mind. "Enterra."

Vaste chewed on his lower lip. "Yes. That would be worse." He started to say something and halted. "I…" The troll's hands clutched his staff, as though he were unsure of how to use it. "I was sorry…about your friend."

When Cyrus did not answer, Vaste began to walk toward the others.

"Vaste," the warrior called. The troll turned, looking back at him. "…thank you."

With a nod and a half smile, Vaste turned and resumed his path back to Brevis. The rain became so loud pounding on his armor that Cyrus could hear nothing at all, and somewhere in the midst of it he fell asleep.

Five

The next day he awoke to the slow sound of droplets falling from the trees. The sharp smell of stagnant water had returned, muted by the previous night's downpour. A chill in the air raised goosepimples on Cyrus's arms and legs.

"Ah, good, you're awake," came the voice of Brevis. His gnarled face hovered into view above Cyrus's eyes, causing the warrior to start.

"You seem more chipper than you were yesterday," Cyrus observed.

"That's because today we collect our gold and go home!" Brevis announced with enthusiasm. His hand pointed in the direction they had been going the day before. "We couldn't see it in the rain."

Cyrus's eyes alighted on yellow stone jutting above the treetops. "That's it?" He judged it to be only a few miles away.

"That's it," Brevis agreed. "Let's go, shall we?"

They broke camp a few minutes later, striding through the jungle with renewed purpose. Soon they reached a clearing and stopped. The temple had a circular base several hundred feet wide, with each subsequent floor comprised of a slightly smaller, fifteen foot high circle stacked on top. Cyrus counted 20 when he hit the topmost ring, which was almost as tall as it was wide.

Cy was reminded of an ornate wedding cake he had once seen in a baker's window in Reikonos. The stone of the temple was a faded yellow and the walls were carved with patterns and glyphs. A set of stairs was carved into the levels in front of them, stretching up to the tenth ring, where an opening stood, imposing and dark.

"Wonderful!" Brevis cried. "This shouldn't take long!"

Vaste edged closer to Cyrus and spoke in a voice no one else could hear. "You seem jumpy."

Cyrus sighed, but the tension did not leave his body. "I know it sounds cowardly and clichéd, but I have a very bad feeling about this place."

Vaste frowned. "You're right – that was clichéd." He looked up at the aperture far above them. "But you're not wrong."

They followed Brevis as the gnome squealed with excitement up the steps. Cyrus noted that each floor, although smaller, left only a foot or two of edge around the temple. He looked back; trying to skip down from the top without using the stairs would be an exceptionally poor idea.

Vaste huffed next to him. "They couldn't have put the entrance on the ground floor?"

At the top, Cyrus looked across the jungle. Ruins dotted the landscape as if there had once been a city in the jungle, but long, long ago. Nothing was left now but remnants.

Brevis sped into the entry without waiting. Cyrus followed a few steps behind, sword drawn out of a sense of caution that he could not define. He heard Vaste's breathing behind him and felt the wind die as they drew down the tunnel. There was a stark silence in front of him save for the gnome's footsteps. The smell of must and stale air wrinkled his nose.

"Light, Aina," Brevis said. A small burst of fire flew along the side of the tunnel, lighting torches as it passed. "Much better."

"Let me help you," Vaste said behind Cyrus. The tunnel lightened further; the troll had cast a spell that gave Cyrus improved night vision.

They passed into a large circular chamber with four sets of steps ringing the walls; two sets leading up and two leading down into the base of the temple. In the center of the room an emblem was carved in the floor, a strange icon of a death's head surrounded by figures; some kneeling, some standing, some dying. Cyrus felt a shudder of discomfort run through him. At the far end of the room an altar was carved into the wall, raised on a dais and sandwiched between the two staircases leading up.

Brevis squeaked. "Where's the gold?" Outrage filtered through his voice. "This place was supposed to be adorned with it!"

"Perhaps it's downstairs?" Vaste suggested.

"Nothing down there but worlds of trouble," a husky voice called from one of the staircases in front of them. "Cultists that used this place before turned it into a catacomb, bodies everywhere." A drawling accent filled Cyrus's ears and he watched a figure descending the stairs. Others came down opposite him, and some rose from behind them, cutting off the exit. They were trolls and every one of them looked lean and rangy, wearing dirty rags and carrying swords and daggers, save for the speaker who wore a gray cloak, clean white gloves and a spotless doublet. Their green skin glistened in the torchlight.

Cyrus could see the leader's dark eyes, his face crisscrossed with scars.

He came down the stairs with a calm assurance that unnerved Cyrus in spite of the leader's hands being free of armament. The cloak moved aside and Cy caught a glimpse of a sword on his belt.

"You're Byb Hirrin," Vaste said.

"You know me?" Byb said, feigning surprise, hand flung mock-dramatically to his breast. "A fan?"

"You know this troll?" Cyrus asked under his breath.

"We're not an exclusive club where all the members know each other," Vaste replied. "I've seen him on a wanted poster in Reikonos. He's a heretic."

Cyrus looked back at the troll leader who wore a grim smile, and a rush of familiarity ran him as he connected the name with a face he had seen on posters.

"I prefer visionary," Byb replied, almost at the bottom of the staircase. Cyrus caught sight of a troll archer standing behind the heretic.

"As I recall," Cyrus said, looking around with a weary tone in his voice, "you were an exiled troll dark knight who captured and tortured members of The Holy Brethren and the Commonwealth of Arcanists, trying to get them to teach you their magic in some bizarre bid to defy nature."

"What can I say?" Byb said with a sardonic look, lips flat. "I got an urge to see if I could cast wizard and paladin spells, and I just couldn't keep myself from giving it a try."

"So you murdered and tortured people?" Cyrus asked. Brevis stood in front of him, looking stunned. Aina was inscrutable as usual but Gertan's constant smile had disappeared.

"Here's the real kick," Byb said with a chuckle, "if I'd just killed and tortured people to sate my own lusts or enrich my wallet, I'd only be wanted in Reikonos, so I could go and live it up in Saekaj Sovar with the dark elves. I hear they like killing and torturing down there; we'd get along. But, no, I went and messed with the Leagues." He shook his head. "Heretic is a name that follows you a long ways, you know? Like…the whole world over."

"Why not go home to Gren?" Cyrus asked. "I hear your kind likes killing and torturing too."

Byb's smile was ironic. "I've been unwelcome there for a long time." His head swung to Vaste. "Probably for the same reason as your young friend here. You should join us," he said with a nod. "We welcome exiles."

"Oh, joy," Vaste commented. "My fondest ambition fulfilled – to find a decrepit temple in the wilderness that I could live in with a band of sadistic killers for the rest of my days." His voice dripped with irony.

"Better than the alternative," Byb purred.

"Is there no gold here?" Brevis asked, voice filled with the last vestiges of hope.

Byb laughed, a booming sound befitting his gargantuan frame. "Nothing here but dead bodies and soon-to-be-dead bodies."

Cyrus did not wait for another word. He swept back with his sword, catching the heretic easing up behind him with a perfect stroke that slit his throat. A quick count revealed that Byb had about ten followers lined around the room – five behind them, blocking the exit, and four descending from above along with Byb. Nine now, Cyrus thought. And all of them are bigger than me, even the females.

With a bellowing warcry, Cyrus lunged forward, brushing Brevis out of the way and launching into the front ranks of enemies before them. He crossed swords with two brigands, a male and a female, while behind him he heard a loud thump and tossed a glance back to see Vaste had seized one of the skinny heretics and hurled him against the wall. The heretic lay bleeding next to Cyrus's first victim, and the other three were keeping their distance from Vaste but still blocking the exit.

Arrows flew past Cyrus's head. "Your archers are pretty sorry to miss at this distance," Cyrus said to Byb, who stood with his arms folded at the base of the left-hand staircase. "Perhaps troll brains aren't large enough for archery."

"It's not wise to insult us," the heretic responded, eyes closed, leaning against the wall with a look of great unconcern. "We might have given you a painless death."

"If they aim a sword as well as they shoot, I doubt it'd be painless."

"Get us out of here, Aina!" Brevis screamed, on his hands and knees.

She nodded and began to cast a spell. A look of panic replaced her normally inscrutable look and she shook her head. "I can't," came her wheezing voice. "Someone's blocking spell casting!"

Cyrus kicked the female heretic off her feet then struck the second with such force that he was knocked back into the wall. Cy darted forward to attack Byb, who sprung from where he leaned, opening his eyes and drawing his sword, a long, black blade.

"Get back here!" Brevis shouted. It took Cyrus a moment to realize that the gnome was talking to him. A slight breeze crossed his face and he turned to see the winds of a teleport spell whipping around his party. Byb's sword blow struck him in the gut, slipping under his armor and drawing his attention back to the fight he was in. The dark knight wore a sly grin as Cyrus pulled away from the wounding strike.

Cy felt hot blood slip down his belly. Judging by the pain, it was deeper than he would have hoped. He staggered back, running into another attack; the male brigand he had knocked over grasped him, locking his arm around Cyrus's neck. The winds of the teleport spell stirred the air around them like a howling tornado had been loosed in the temple.

Must…get…back…

Reversing his grip, Cyrus plunged the sword down, through the joint of the brigand's knee. A scream of pain and he relinquished his grip. The winds were at a fever pitch now, vortex filling the air as Cyrus leapt forward just as the teleport spell was cast and the tornado died; his last view of his party was Brevis's wrinkled face, twisting and distorting behind the curtains of the wind as it swept out of existence.

Six

"Courageous bunch you run with," Byb said with a grin. Cyrus looked over his shoulder and pulled back to his feet, turning to face the dark knight and the enemies that moved forward with him. The archers had their bows raised, arrows notched and pointed. This time it was unlikely they would miss. The circle of green faces around him was a mass of unbroken smiles as they edged closer to him.

He backed up and bumped into a solid wall. With alarm, he looked back to see Vaste standing, back against his. He felt a warm touch course against his belly wound as the troll cast a healing spell on him. "It would appear we're against some dramatic odds here," Vaste observed.

"I don't favor your chances," Byb drawled. "Eight against two? Why don't you give up now and we can hash out what's to be done with you."

"Why?" Vaste asked. "Fancy the idea of torturing a healer to try to learn his magic as well?"

"Seems pointless," Cyrus commented, "since he's a dark knight and can only learn the spells of a dark knight."

Byb's grin grew wider. "That noble effort at experimenting – that's what makes me a heretic."

"And the torture and murder?" Cyrus gazed at the troll's dark eyes and saw pools of uncaring, a reflection of everything he'd ever known about trolls. *He would kill us and anyone that came after us, and not lose a wink of sleep over it.*

"It's fun," the heretic replied. "You want to hear how I got started on that? See, I survived the battle of Thurren Hill, when Quinneria killed ten thousand of us with a single spell, and I had this crazy idea—"

Vaste pushed back from Cyrus, causing the warrior to stumble forward. He swung his sword in a clumsy swipe at the enemies in front of him, causing them to take a step back. He shot an angry look at Vaste, who had used his massive frame to knock back three of the enemies behind them. Two others circled to block the door. Arrows sunk into the back of the Healer, who let loose a roar of outrage and charged down the staircase behind them. "COME ON!" he shouted.

Cyrus did not need to be told twice. He took another swing at the approaching heretics and ran for the staircase. He followed Vaste, taking the steps two and three at a time. Torches burned ahead of him, and he saw the healer's bulky figure cut to the right around a corner.

"There's no way out from down there!" Byb's voice called. "Get comfortable; we'll wait for you up here. When you're ready, come on out. If the human is dead, that's even better." A round of guffaws could be heard echoing in the catacombs. "He looks meaty. He'll make a good dinner."

Cyrus stopped and looked back around the corner. There was no sign of pursuit. "Do you believe him?"

"About you being a good dinner? I doubt it; you're too lean; I like some fat on my meat—"

Cyrus glared through the dark. "About there being no way out."

"Oh. Yeah. I believe him."

"Can't we just use your return spell to escape to Sanctuary?"

Silence hung between them as Vaste raised his hand and rested it on the back of his head. "We could. If I knew that spell."

"You don't know the return spell?" Cyrus hissed. "I thought every magic user got taught it in League training!"

Vaste shrugged. "My training was somewhat unconventional." He shifted his gaze downward. "I'll learn it when we get back. I've been meaning to for a while, but when you always travel with wizards and druids it seems unnecessary."

"Figures." Cyrus's voice was low and malicious. "I get saddled with the only healer in Sanctuary that doesn't know how to cast a return spell – and you're just like them: a…" His hands gesticulated, pointing at Vaste in accusation.

"A what?" Vaste spat back. "A troll?"

"A savage!"

"Says the man with the blood-covered sword! Brilliant, dumbass. Because I'm a troll I'm automatically a savage? You're ignorant – and not because you're human, but because you're a damned ignorant idiot!"

"Your whole race is savages. Everybody knows it. Slavers and savages; it's why the humans and the elves went to war against you twenty years ago!" The adrenaline was coursing through Cyrus's veins and his words were flowing faster now, no care to what he was saying.

"You think I'm like them?" He waved at the entrance to the catacombs.

"Do you blame me for your father's death too?" Vaste looked at Cyrus, the torchlight reflecting in his dark eyes, specks of brown shining in them. "Oh, yes, Orion told me – your father died in the war with my people. Congratulations!" A sneer crossed the troll's face, his lips twisted. "I hate to tell you this, but I was your age during the war, because all I remember of it was the day my mother and father died, and the outrage and public mourning when we surrendered."

"And did you mourn too?" Cyrus snapped. "Did you pound your chest with all the other trolls? Rejoice in human deaths like all the others?"

"Of course I did." Vaste's calmness unnerved him. "I was four years old and I had lost my parents. I went along with the crowd; it's not like I had the capacity to make up my own mind yet. In fact, I didn't really make up my own mind until long after I left the troll homeland."

Vaste's finger reached out, resting light on the front of Cyrus's breastplate. "I could sit around and bemoan fate and get bitter about all I've lost every day for the rest of my life. Most trolls do; they wake up and spend their days grousing about how much their life sucks and how they went from being citizens of the largest and most powerful nation in Arkaria to being refugees living in tent cities in a swamp, and every night they go to bed with a complaint on their lips. I wanted more; and I'm smarter than most of them – smarter than you as well, by the appearance of things."

"You think so?"

"Well, we're outnumbered in the middle of a temple filled with troll heretics who would let me freely join them if I killed you, and you seem to want to piss off the only person in this temple that would like to see you live, so you tell me – how smart are you?" Vaste crossed his arms, staring down at the human warrior.

Dammit. He's right. "Fine, we'll settle this later."

"Settle what?" Vaste asked. "Settle my stupidity for assisting you at every turn? Settle my idiocy for trying to make nice with you even though you have constantly rebuffed my every attempt to be friendly? Settle my entire people's debt for killing your father in the war?"

"I don't know – we'll talk about it later!" Cyrus replied.

"Talk about what?!" Vaste shouted at him. "Do you think I would sell you out to them to save my own skin? Do you think *I* killed your father?"

"YES!" Cyrus shouted back, last reserve of fury breaking loose. "You and your whole treacherous, violent, brutal race!"

A silence hung in the air between them as Cyrus took a moment to compose himself. He struggled to catch his breath while Vaste stared him down. "You're still alive, Davidon. I haven't betrayed you."

"Yet." The words came with a bitter, acrid tone that burned his tongue.

"I've extended the hand of friendship at every turn and you've slapped it away," Vaste said. "Now we're alone in the jungle, surrounded by enemies, and you want to count me among them. What is it going to take?" Vaste shook his head, a look of incredulity in his eyes. "You told me when we met that you would judge me based on my actions and not my race. I have extended courtesy after courtesy and had you throw them back in my face! I've judged you based on those words and not your actions, and you have judged me by lumping me in with those vile murderers up there!" Vaste's long finger wagged at the corridor they had entered from. "I'm not them! You might have been right about those trolls, but you're wrong about me!"

Cyrus stood still, the lack of air movement causing his skin to crawl. He watched Vaste, stonefaced, unmoving before him, anger spent. He heard light laughter in the distance from the staircases and tasted the bile in his mouth as his mind replayed his every act of unkindness toward Vaste. "I'm sorry." The shame crept over him. "You're right."

"Now that we've gotten that out of the way," Vaste replied, "let's make a plan to deal with them. We can take them out and walk out of here – together."

I don't know that I want to, Cyrus thought. "You have been decent to me since we met – and I've been..." He took a deep breath. "...not so gracious. If we can make it to the entrance tunnel, I can hold them all off while you get away – maybe even take enough of them out that they won't want to follow you. I'll cover your retreat and join you when I'm finished." *And maybe soon I'll see Narstron again.*

"You'll be dead," Vaste replied. "Byb is a dark knight and he has nasty magics at his command – tunnel or not, he'll slaughter you from a distance with his spell casting ability. I can keep you healed."

"There are at least eight of them," Cyrus said with a shake of the head. "The odds are against us. They are bigger than me – and some of them are stronger."

"But if they're coming at you in the tunnel, it's one-on-one or one-on-two. Those are good odds for us with you in front – your skill with a sword is far beyond any of theirs. And you've got an expert healer backing you up. They get wounded, die and stay dead." The troll cracked a smile. "That evens the odds."

"Fine," Cyrus agreed, tired of arguing. Exhaustion filled him and he wanted the fight to be over. "Let's give it a try. But be ready to run if things turn ugly."

Vaste's eyes flickered in the dark. "I'm not a coward that's concerned with saving my own hide above all else; I'm a member of Sanctuary and I stand and fight beside my guildmates." He arched an eyebrow at Cyrus. "Even the ignorant ones."

"Loyalty," Cyrus said with a downward look.

"Surprised to find it from a troll?"

Cyrus's eyes traced the lines around his boots. "We should go. Vaste?" Cyrus said.

"Yes?"

Cyrus froze. "When you get back to Sanctuary, please don't tell anyone about...what I said here."

Vaste stared him down, bending to look him in the eyes. "If you survive, I won't. But if you do something asinine to get yourself killed, I'll tell everyone what a moron you were." Cyrus's eyes snapped up, inward fire burning as Vaste stared him down. "This isn't your chance to redeem your ignorance by dying a hero. I don't care how much you're drowning in despair from what happened in Enterra or if you feel like a stupid wretch for espousing ignorant dogmas; this is your chance to learn and change – and not be a zealot who has to hide from living in the world his whole life."

"What I said is unforgivable."

"Not unless you continue believing it."

Cyrus led the way, easing toward the staircase. None of the heretics were in sight when they reached the bottom of the steps. "Let's try and catch them by surprise."

"I'll be right behind you," Vaste whispered back.

From above, a peal of laughter rang out over quiet conversation. Cyrus knew that at least two of the enemies had their backs to the staircase from their laughter, and they were close by. *If I can get those two first, it'll help our chances...*

He climbed the stairs slowly, taking a step at a time and being careful not to clank his metal boots on the stone. He saw two of the brigands – the male and female that had assaulted him earlier, both standing with their backs to the stairs, unaware of his presence.

He jumped the last couple steps and reached up, grabbing each of them by an ankle, yanking with all his weight. Twin cries echoed as they lost their footing and were dragged down by Cyrus. The male tried to grab the ledge and failed, his jaw breaking on it as he passed. He crumpled to Cyrus's feet, unconscious, a thin line of blood running out of his mouth.

The female, by virtue of faster reflexes, managed to catch the ledge as she fell. Cyrus reached up and grabbed her around the waist. His hand slithered up to her stomach and ripped loose her fragile hold, slamming her to the stairs below with a thunderous crack of breaking bones. He could feel the shock of her impact and watched as she went limp and lifeless, her corpse sliding down the stairs.

Shouts filled the air above him as he charged up the remaining steps. There was no one between him and the entrance tunnel now. Vaste followed only a step behind, and Cyrus interposed himself between the healer and the remaining six heretics.

"It would appear you're without a healer, Byb." Cyrus smirked at the sight of the bodies of the two they had downed earlier, lying off to the side of the chamber.

"Indeed," returned the dark knight, no amusement on his face. "It's why I was hoping your comrade would be willing to betray you."

"I'm afraid I must decline," Vaste's deep voice boomed. "I make an effort not to be seen in the company of swine such as yourself."

"A blood traitor, huh?" Byb's smile cracked his serious expression. "Too good for your own people?"

"Too good for you," Vaste said with a smile.

"A diet of his toejam would be too good for you," Cyrus replied.

"My toejam?" Vaste said, sotto voce. "That's fairly graphic. And inaccurate – I'll have you know I wash my feet regularly—"

"Shush," Cyrus said as they backed down the tunnel.

Byb's archers had moved into position, flanking the dark knight. "You know," Byb said, "I think we're about to see you riddled with arrows."

"Only if your archers have gotten better with their aim than last round," Cyrus shot back. As if to answer him, two arrows shot at him, both glancing off his armor – one at the chest, one at his shoulder. "It would appear they have not. Maybe if they stood right next to me and held the arrow to my head...?"

"Laugh while you can." Byb's voice turned easy, genial. "It's a long tunnel."

Cyrus paused. "Good point."

Without telegraphing his intentions, Cyrus charged. Although unlikely to match the strength of the trolls, his speed was greater. Two more arrows bounced from his armor, one skipping the seam where his forearm plate met his gauntlet. He closed the distance before the archers could bring another volley to bear.

Sidestepping Byb, who had drawn his sword, Cyrus plunged his blade into the first archer, who had thrown his bow aside to draw a dagger but failed to free it from the scabbard in time.

Byb swung at Cyrus but the slice went wide as the warrior sidestepped, lowered his shoulder and lunged, knocking Byb back a few steps. "You can't stop me," the dark knight spouted as Vaste's staff came down from behind and clipped him in the back of the head. Byb fell to his knees, clutching the base of his skull.

Cyrus did not halt his attack, slinging his sword around in an arc in front of him as he took a step toward the second archer. This one had freed his dagger, but the blade was too high to react to Cyrus's attack. The warrior's sword stabbed through the troll's canvas shirt and Cy kicked the archer to free his blade from where it had lodged between the heretic's ribs.

Cy did a quick assessment of the situation. With Byb on the ground and the two archers dead, it left only three heretics. One walked with a pronounced limp from where Cyrus had impaled his knee earlier; one of the others was attacking Vaste, who was holding her back with his staff, her rapier clicking against the hard wood. With a last flourish, Vaste struck her hand, sending the sword skittering across the floor, then brought the staff around and knocked her to her knees. He struck her a final time across the back of the neck and she slumped to the ground.

Cyrus looked at the two that he faced – one limping and the other lean and rangy, a worried look in his eyes. The one with perfect mobility kept out of arm's reach, bringing a smile to Cyrus's face. He lunged and raked his sword across the troll's neck; a perfectly aimed strike that dropped the heretic with a single hit, hands shaking as they tried in to control the geyser of blood welling from his throat. The one that limped held his sword in front of him as though it were a shield and circled away from Cyrus.

"It would appear the odds have evened," Cyrus taunted the brigand, whose shaggy black hair hung over his face, eyes wide and looking down at Cyrus in fear and anticipation of an attack. *Just need to circle him a bit more...* "I bet you didn't see things turning out quite this way."

Cyrus had turned him so the limping brigand was hobbling back now, in retreat, so scared of the warrior that he paid no attention to Vaste, who was standing behind him. He bumped into the healer, turned in fright with sword raised to strike and Cyrus closed and yanked him by the ragged collar, impaling him through the chest. The heretic's sword clattered to the stone and Vaste watched with impassive eyes as he fell to the ground.

"Byb?" Cyrus asked.

Vaste shrugged. "I got distracted."

They turned to see the dark knight standing in front of the entrance tunnel. "Boys, you've cleaned out my hideout. I'm gonna have to relocate myself to somewhere choicer."

"You think you'll make it out the door?" Cyrus asked, now smiling like Byb. A gripping pain slammed into his chest, an agony as intense as if someone had stabbed him through the heart with a sword. He dropped to a knee, gasping.

"I reckon I'll be all right," Byb replied with a smirk. "I'm not planning to go back to Reikonos with you, that's for sure. They're lying to everybody about how magic works." His eyes were deadened as he spoke, a haunted look passing over him. "And when you find out their secrets, they call you a heretic."

"Says the troll who delights in the slaughter and pain of others," Vaste retorted. "Thanks for giving the rest of us a bad name."

"Embrace it," Byb said, mouth twisted. "Humans and all these other mortals are so small, so flimsy. Trolls were made to rule them. There's another war coming, and our people will need us. There's no mad sorceress to stop us this time. If we just embrace the magics of our heritage..." He glared down at Vaste. "Everything I've done is for us. Our kind. They need us! They will welcome us back as heroes! In a land without magic...we are gods!"

"You're no god," Vaste pronounced.

Byb smiled. "Someday you'll see it my way. And I'll be there to say 'I told you so'. It's been a joy. Although you've killed my clan, you did liven up a dull stay out here." He tipped an imaginary hat in salute.

"I'll find my joy in bringing your head back to Reikonos," Cyrus growled at him, pain subsiding in his chest.

Byb smiled, a wide grin aimed at Cyrus. "I think we'll cross swords again." He started to run down the tunnel.

Cyrus snatched Vaste's staff out of the healer's hands and sprung after Byb. His legs pounded as he ran down the tunnel and hurled it like a javelin. It flew between Byb's legs as the heretic ran through the open entryway and began to descend the stairs. His shin connected with the staff and it snagged his foot. He stumbled, twisting as he fell sideways off the temple. Cyrus watched as he disappeared, arms flailing, black eyes wide.

Cyrus chewed his lip for a moment and pondered the drop. "I think not."

"You better not have broken my staff," Vaste said, annoyed. "It's mystical."

"Then it's doubtful that some skinny troll tripping over it and dropping it a few hundred feet is going to break it, right?"

"You better hope."

"If it's broken, the two hundred thousand gold pieces we're about to collect should buy a new one."

"Two hundred thousand?" Vaste frowned.

"Yeah," Cyrus replied, "A hundred for him, ten for each of his cronies. They're all heretics."

Vaste's eyes glazed over. "Two hundred thousand gold…that's more than we would have gotten from Brevis's treasure…"

"Especially after he deducted his percentage." Cyrus smiled. "Fifty-fifty, right?"

"Well, if I had to become a bounty hunter and split money with any ignorant savage, I'm pleased it was you." His frown dissolved, making way for a crooked grin across his face.

"Well, I'm aspiring to become more than that."

"Keep working on it," Vaste told him with a pat on the shoulder. "I'll let you know when you've arrived."

They followed the long staircase down to find Byb's body crumpled at the base of the temple. The bandit's green face was slack, his neck at an impossible angle, Vaste's staff lying a few feet away. Cyrus picked it up, dusted it off and handed it to Vaste. "Seems fine."

The troll looked at it with suspicion, eyes scouring it. "It could be damaged. The crystal could be cracked. I want an expert opinion."

Cyrus yanked it out of the healer's hands and peered at it, inspecting every inch with a weathered eye before tossing it back. "Flawless. Now quit griping."

"How do we collect these bounties?" Vaste asked. "Do we have to carry the bodies back to Reikonos?"

"Not the whole body, no…"

A hint of pleading ran through Vaste's voice. "I don't do decapitations."

"Fine, you elf-girl. I'll do it."

"Don't let Vara hear you call anyone that."

Cyrus drew his sword and finished in a few cuts, turning back to Vaste when he was done. The troll's skin held a greener hue than usual and he almost stammered as he spoke. "I've seen that done during battles – you know, a good, sure slice. Even during an execution or two. But…that was brutal."

"Yeah," Cyrus said with a grin of obvious enjoyment at the troll's discomfort. "I've got to go back up and get the rest, and I'll need someone to hold the bag."

"Pass."

"This is a vital part of collecting the bounty!" Cyrus's grin deepened to what he was certain could only be described as evil.

"Still pass. Saving your ass was a vital enough part of collecting the bounty for me. Way to work on overcoming your savagery."

"My savagery is about to make us a lot of money." The grin faded as Cyrus looked at the healer, clearly ill at the thought of the gore involved. "I'll take care of it," Cyrus promised. "Wait for me here."

Vaste rolled his eyes. "Well I'm not going to stalk off into the jungle by myself and leave the bounties behind. Or you."

The ascent to the entrance of the temple seemed half as high with the battle won. Cyrus found a knapsack carried by one of the heretics and dealt with them one by one. The red blood stood in contrast to the green skin of the trolls and began to pool in the cracks of the old floor, running toward the carved symbol in the middle of it. Cyrus had finished with the last of them, taking care to raid their purses before he left, and cinched the knapsack when a low hissing filled his ears.

A slight shiver ran down his spine and his eyes darted around, looking for the source of the noise. He looked to all sides and clutched his sword in one hand. A voice filled the air, emanating from the space around the raised altar. **"I am...the Avatar of the God of Death...of Mortus. You have brought me sacrifices..."**

Cyrus blinked in alarm, edging toward the door. "Uh...you're welcome?"

"For a hundred years my followers worshipped here...extolling the glory of death...until he came...trapping me in the darkness...but you...have freed me with the blood of sacrifice..."

Cyrus did not see anything in the darkness before him. An indescribable feeling of dread clutched at him, driving a fear unlike any he had ever felt. He cast a look back. *Almost to the door. Don't know if that counts for anything, but hopefully I can get away.* "Again, you're welcome."

"Need...more blood to bring...the personification of Death...to Arkaria..."

"Well," Cyrus said with a gulp, clutching the bag of heads in his hand, "those bodies are still draining, so you'll continue to have a fair supply for a while." *Almost there...*

"Need more...fresh...blood..."

"I might be able to help you with that...there's another troll outside...let me get him for you..."

"Yes...you are my servant...bring me fresh blood...feed my master's mark...make me strong...free me..."

"Sure. I'll be back in a few minutes." Cyrus had reached the aperture and turned, running full force down the steps, taking them five at a time.

Vaste looked up at him from a seated position on a log, face filled with curiosity. "What? Dead trolls didn't scare you, did they?"

"Run, you jackass! I'll explain later!"

Cyrus tore into the jungle at top speed. A scream of unearthly fury filled the air, radiating from the top of the pyramid, and Cyrus heard Vaste's heavy footfalls only a few steps behind him. "WHAT DID YOU DO?!" the healer shouted as they tore through the jungle along the faint path that they had followed coming in.

"Apparently I brought the blood of sacrifices to the Avatar of the God of Death!"

Vaste's voice was incredulous. "Why would you go and do something like that?"

"It wasn't intentional, and if you weren't such a weak-kneed elf you'd have been helping me do it, so shut up!"

"Can we outrun it?" Vaste's voice was edged with concern and fear.

Cyrus puffed, legs hammering at the soft jungle soil. "If not we can fight it when we get sick of running."

"Great, and we'll be tired out; just the condition I want to be in for a battle with some epic evil!"

They ran for hours, long past the fall of night. Every noise that found their ears sounded like the approach of the ancient death that Cyrus had heard in the temple. Even the normal sounds of the jungle took on a wicked whisper, like a demon stalking their steps. When daybreak came, they had left the jungle path and had been following the road back toward the beach for several hours.

"I don't…know how much…longer I can…run…" Vaste said, breath coming in a sad, wheezing pant, his run slowed to an exhausted jog.

"Yeah…I think we should…rest," Cyrus agreed. "You take first watch."

"I'm not taking first watch; I've been running all night!"

"So have I! And I had to decapitate the damned heretics," he said, waving the bag of heads in front of Vaste's face, "and you trolls have really thick necks!"

"Screw you, I'm sleeping," Vaste said and laid his head down. Heavy, not quite genuine snores filled the air seconds later, replaced in a few minutes by the real thing.

"Fine, let the Avatar of Death sneak up on us in our sleep," Cyrus muttered, eyes darting back and forth.

Vaste awoke several hours later, and Cyrus was eating cold salted beef. "We should get moving again," the warrior said, "so eat fast."

"Did you sleep?"

"No," Cyrus said with a shake of the head. "And I doubt I will until we get back to Sanctuary – which I may never leave again."

"The world will be all the poorer for the loss of your gentle spirit – oh, wait, you don't have one of those."

"Shut up."

They began their journey again, walking this time, following the road as it loped. Cyrus couldn't help but cast a worried glance back every few seconds for the first miles, especially as darkness began to fall.

"I don't think it's coming," Vaste assured him.

"I hope not," Cyrus replied. "I didn't even see it, whatever it was…but it just…gave off an aura of being scary as hell. It was unlike anything I've ever felt."

"You're not usually one to run, are you?"

Cyrus thought about it, realizing for the first time that he had run away from the temple. "No. No, I'm not. Damn." He turned, the cold feeling in his guts replaced with a hot, burning sensation of humiliation. "Damn. Now I have to go back."

"Are you insane?" Vaste asked, eyebrow cocked in disbelief.

"No." Cyrus shook his head. "In the Society of Arms, where I learned to be a warrior, they teach you that you don't run from fear, or you'll have to look over your shoulder for the rest of your life." A deep, biting anger filled him. "I can't believe I did that. I never run unless ordered!"

"I know this is an alien concept, but let's use reason for a moment," Vaste said in a soothing voice. "Why did you run?"

Cyrus frowned, his stomach churning. "It…it spoke to me. I couldn't see it, but I could hear it… and there was something… about that voice. Disembodied, vicious, bloodthirsty… something told me to run."

"That was your common sense. Heed it."

"But what if I could have beaten it? What if we could have killed that thing?"

"Do you know what an Avatar is?" Vaste scoffed. "It's the persona of a god in a form that allows it to be present in Arkaria. It's the nearest thing to taking on a god, short of a trip to their realm. Do you want to fight a god?"

"Maybe," Cyrus replied. "But not today. Not by ourselves. Not…now."

"Yes," Vaste agreed. "Not now. Not ever, in my case. But I applaud your audacity. Some would call it stupidity, but I now consider myself your friend and I will call it audacity just to spare your feelings."

Cyrus ignored the troll's offer of friendship, turning his eyes downward. "I appreciate you sugarcoating your words to spare my foolish pride. And for not betraying me to…them."

Vaste shrugged, massive shoulders causing his head to tilt, peaceful smile on his face. "It's us against 'them'. A friend could do no less."

"Indeed." Cyrus couldn't help but return the troll's magnanimous smile. "A friend could not. Thank you. For saving my life…and forgiving my ignorance."

"You're welcome." The troll's toothy grin stretched from ear to ear. "Besides, they would have probably forced me to eat one of your haunches, and frankly that's just not appealing to me."

The next two days passed quickly, and by the time they reached the beach, Cyrus had stopped looking back at all. Upon reaching the sandy shores, he stared at the Sea of Carmas. "I think I'm going for a swim. I need to wash the stink of this jungle off me."

"Really? The smell reminds me of home." Vaste frowned. "On second thought, I can't wait to wash it off."

"Hold that thought," Cyrus said, looking to the north. Moving along the beach was a host, a line of figures, a few miles away and moving toward them. "An army?"

"Perhaps," Vaste agreed. "See the one in front – female, walking on air?"

Cyrus squinted, looking at who Vaste was pointing to. Even at this distance he could see her, slightly above the others, and atop her head was a tousle of red hair. "Niamh?"

"Indeed." The troll's smile reappeared. "It would seem we have warranted a rescue party."

The Army of Sanctuary moved down the beach toward them, and they waited and waved at their would-be rescuers. As they came into view, Cyrus could see Brevis at the front, fretting next to Niamh, who wore a look of surprised relief. Terian was visible, a knowing smile on his face as he shook his head at the sight of them – as well as Andren, muttering and shaking his finger at Cyrus.

Cyrus saw Vara as well, up front at first, but upon sighting them she sunk to the back of the group, disappearing in its depths. Cheers and well wishes came as they were embraced by the rescue party. Alaric was there too, with a smile peeking out from bottom his metal helm, cut so it left his mouth exposed. "Gentlemen," he greeted them. "I am pleased to see that reports of your demise were premature."

"They weren't far off," Cyrus answered the Ghost, shaking the bag with the heads in it. "But we killed the heretics."

Alaric nodded. "Of course. I would expect no less from the two of you."

Brevis forced his way up to them from next to Alaric, almost falling over himself. "Glad to see you both. So sorry about leaving you behind; if I'd only known…"

Cyrus looked at the gnome with a fading sense of indignation. "We're fine. That's all that matters."

Andren made his way through the crowd, grabbing hold of Cyrus by the shoulders and shaking him. "You leave…no warning, no word, and you go and get your damned fool self left behind! You're gonna put me in an early grave…" The elf's face was a wreck, relief cascading across it along with emotions that normally did not make their way across the elf's facade. "I can't…not you too," he said, looking Cyrus in the eyes. "Not you too, you understand?"

"I understand," Cyrus replied, patting Andren's arm. "But in fairness, Vaste got his 'damned fool self' left behind too."

"Quite the act of courage, my friend," Alaric said, turning to the troll. "Brevis told us you jumped out of the teleportation spell just as it was about to take you out of there."

Cyrus felt a jolt of shock run down his spine. His jaw hung open and he stared, mouth agape, at the troll. "You did that on purpose?"

"What can I say?" Vaste replied, reaching out and placing his arm around Cyrus's shoulder. "I couldn't leave you to face those trolls on your own. After all," he said, a twinkle in his eye, "you really didn't know a thing about them."

A FAMILIAR FACE

Note: This story takes place during **Avenger: The Sanctuary Series, Volume Two**, in the opening pages of Chapter 7, in the weeks before the invasion of the Realm of Darkness.

The wind of a teleportation spell dispersed around Cyrus Davidon. The clink of his armor settling reached his ears, and the smell of home filled his nose. The Great Square of Reikonos appeared before his eyes, with the fountain spraying water above its wide pool and eight tiers of ornate construction. Humans flitted in and out of shops around the massive square and a throng of hundreds of people passed through on the main avenues and side streets.

A hum filled the air, the sound of a thousand voices around him; haggling, talking, shouting and laughing. Horses drank around the fountain, children ran through the streets playing, while vendors accosted the passersby from their street carts, selling wares. Meats hung from strings on stands and the aroma of good food hung heavy in the air.

It was a crisp, early autumn day. Vegetable sellers displayed the last remains of the harvest's freshness, with ears of corn, leeks, tomatoes and potatoes pushed to the front of their stands. Jewelry of cheaper varieties was present as well, along with some metalwork and leather items.

The high voice of Niamh, a red-haired druid, broke through the commotion around them. "Any chance you can just get what you need here in the square and we can be on our way back to Sanctuary?" Short, with bright eyes and a broad smile, which she displayed now, she could control the currents of magic to teleport from location to location across the world of Arkaria.

"I won't be long," Cyrus replied. "You have things you could be doing, I trust?"

"Mmm..." She chewed on her lip as she thought about it. "I could...maybe go play with the kids around the fountain."

He stared across the square where a few human children splashed water on each other while their mothers filled buckets from the fountain. He looked back at her. "How old are you again?"

"Six hundred and—"

"Never mind," he muttered. "Meet you back here when I'm done?"

"Okay." She wandered toward the fountain, slinking in a way that led him to believe that she was planning to do some splashing, and he shook his head in amazement.

The truth was that Cyrus had no real need to shop; none of the blacksmiths in town had a sword and that was all he required at present. Sanctuary, the guild that gave him food and lodging, provided for almost all of his material needs, leaving him wanting for little else. *No,* he thought, *this is just the kind of day when I need to get out of Sanctuary for a while and stretch my legs.* He smiled. *And maybe I needed to see the old hometown.*

The streets became more packed as he walked, the side streets off the square beckoning him onward, toward the old market. *I wonder why,* he thought. *I haven't been through this part of the city in a while.*

The buildings grew faded as he went on, and they spaced out; the square was lined with shops next door to one another that gave way to more and more stalls and stands as he went deeper into the market. Vendors haggled with their customers over all variety of wares, many even odder than the commonplace items found in the square. Eel eyes sat in a prominent place on one stand, next to various herbs and other strong foliage. *Alchemy,* Cyrus thought. *Such an interesting art.* Another stand promised dragonmeat. After stopping and staring, Cyrus suspected it was merely the haunch of a goat, cut and seared in an odd shape.

He walked down the row until one stand caught his eye. Flowers sprouted from it, all different shapes and shades, from mundane – dandelions – to the extraordinary – a glowrose. The light sparkled off its petals, shimmering in a thousand different colors, as though a rainbow had been woven beneath the skin of the flower.

A woman carried a vase filled with a dozen of the more common red roses from behind the stand. Her hair was dark and fell to mid-back, and her olive skin carried a deep tint that reminded Cyrus of the rich wood that

Sanctuary's furniture was made of. She wore a dress of deep red, and her apron and heavy gloves told him she worked at the stand. She caught sight of him as he passed and halted in surprise, as though she hadn't seen him approach. "Hello," she said cautiously. "How do you do?"

"I'm well," he replied, stopping his forward progress to check her wares. *No harm in being polite,* he thought. "And yourself?"

"Much the same." Her words came out stiff, unnatural, somewhat forced. "What brings you by my stall on such a fine day?"

"Just taking a walk." He forced a smile, and thought she had a familiar face, but he couldn't place it.

"I haven't seen you in the markets for quite some time," she said. She smiled, but it was tight, as though she were putting a great deal of effort into it.

He felt a prick of embarrassment at not being able to place her. *Do I know her?* he wondered. *Should I admit to her I can't remember her name or where I know her from?* He faked a smile as he looked over her cart. *A flower seller; she must know me because of Imina.*

He felt a pang of guilt; Imina had been his wife for two years. She also sold flowers in the Reikonos market; it was a community of sorts, with fierce competition, but within bounds. She always came home smelling of sweetness and dirt at the end of the day, and he took deep breaths, enjoying the scent of both when he buried his face in her long, luxuriant hair. They had parted ways after he refused to give up the life of a guild warrior. "I haven't been around much," he answered. "I live at the Sanctuary guildhall now."

"I see." She folded her hands over her belly, as though she were nervous and didn't know what to do with them. Something about the way she did it struck him as odd. "I'd heard a rumor that a dashing young warrior clad all in black armor ran afoul of the old Dragonlord, Ashan'agar. That he fought him in single combat and killed him in a brutal showdown." She turned away for a moment and walked to the side of the cart, then looked back at him as she pulled out a scissor and cut a rose at the stem, placing it in a vase. "Then I heard a different rumor that suggested that the guild Goliath had been responsible for killing the Dragonlord, not the warrior in black." She looked up at him, and her eyes were focused and bored into his. "I decided I liked the second story better."

He reddened. "I've heard that rumor myself. Didn't much care for the

Goliath version; it smacks of lies."

She stared at him, not breaking eye contact, her chin up, before she deflated slightly and looked down to the roses she was cutting. "I figured as much. But I still like it better."

Cyrus looked at the glowrose, its petals gleaming in the light of the sun. "Those were my wife's favorite flower." He coughed. "My former wife," he corrected.

She looked up at him with a slight glitter in her eyes and said, "I know."

He nodded and picked up one of them gently, to avoid crushing it in his armored fingers. "Do you see her – my lady wife – often?"

She looked up at him, regarding him carefully. "Every day," she answered after a pause.

"Is she well?"

The flower girl returned to her work. "Well enough. She misses you."

He looked away, not sure of how to respond. He had a memory of Imina, before the hard times had set in, of being in bed with her on a lazy day, begging her not to go to the stand, to just stay with him. She'd smiled and hemmed and hawed, but eventually left...perhaps a little later than expected, but she'd gone nonetheless.

He smelled the sweet scent of the flowers and brought the glowrose up to his nose. Although she sold them, she'd never had one of her own. A product of elven gardens, glowroses were exceptionally rare and expensive, and Cyrus had never had enough money to buy her one. She'd always demurred and said she saw them all day at work, but he'd seen the way she stared at them, longing. *Would things have gone differently for us if I'd taken a job as a Reikonos guard and bought her a glowrose of her own every now and again? Or would I have been so miserable, chafing under that life, that I'd have taken it out on her?*

"Sir?" The flower girl stirred him out of his lapse. He looked back at her, the pretty face staring at him. "I must ask you...in your adventures, have you died?"

"Aye. A few times now." He laughed. "Don't tell Imina." He held the stem between his fingers and stared at the glowrose. It was truly beautiful, and of all the things he regretted, not ever having enough money to buy Imina one was probably the biggest regret of them all. He turned serious.

"You said you see her every day. Will you see her yet this day?"

She turned her eyes to the task she was undertaking. "Yes. I will."

He opened the coinpurse on his belt and pulled several gold coins, setting them on the cart in front of her. It was likely more than she made in a week, even if she sold a glowrose or two. "Give the glowrose to her, when next you see," he told her, handing it back. "I owe her this much, at least."

She took it with an outstretched hand, the gold glaring in the sunlight against the dull cloth of her glove, her face registering a stunned reaction. "I...I...I can't take this..." She stared at the gold.

"Then give it to her as well," he said, cinching the coinpurse shut and turning away. A heady rush of emotion threatened to overwhelm him, and he walked away, ignoring the calls of the flower girl as he strode through the market.

I haven't thought of Imina in years. He brushed past a vendor hawking carpets as another memory bubbled up.

"I don't complain about how much time you spend at your stand," he said, lying in bed, watching her dress.

Her green eyes glared at him as she cinched a belt around her narrow waist. It hung on her hips, which curved wonderfully out in a way he couldn't take his eyes away from, especially when she was undressed. "Working at my flower stand doesn't seem likely to end in my death." She sat down on the bed next to him and ran a hand over his rough cheek, her ring glittering with a beautiful emerald green light. The ring was the only possession they'd had that was worth anything, other than his armor. The light flooded in from the single window of their rented apartment. "If you ever join one of these big guilds, you may die."

He stretched and sat up, wrapping his arms around her, his naked flesh pressed against the soft cloth of her dress. "They have healers. They can cast a resurrection spell that will bring me back."

"It doesn't always work that way." She shrugged out of his arms. "Not everyone comes back; guilds lose people all the time. Sometimes even a whole guild gets wiped out on an adventure, and then there's no one to bring you back!" She wore the pouty expression, the one that came before an argument. "And even if they do bring you back, I've heard the stories; you're never quite the same after a resurrection spell. You lose memories, and you don't even know what they are."

He sighed. "I've heard that too," he admitted. "But we don't need to worry about it," he said, tugging at the hem of her dress, "because I'm not going to die." He shot her his most endearing smile and pulled her back onto the bed. She let out a squeal of surprise as he rolled on top of her and brought his mouth to hers. She ran a hand through his long hair, her soft lips playing against his. When they broke away, he stared into her eyes. "I'm not going to die."

She chewed her lower lip and played with a strand of his hair. "Promise?"

"I promise." He smiled and kissed her again.

He walked past a blacksmith's stand without even noticing or caring. *I was such a fool,* he thought. *That wasn't a promise I could make.* The argument, short as it was, became the first of many. *An unrelenting sore spot,* Cyrus thought, *along with my lack of money.* He shuddered as he came out of a shaded alleyway and entered Reikonos Square. The fountain was ahead of him, and he quickened his pace.

Niamh was waiting, laughing and splashing water from the fountain's edge at some children nearby. She stood up when she saw him. He heard a voice behind him, calling his name, and turned. The flower girl was hurrying behind, her hand outstretched, gold lying on her now-bare palm. *She wants to give me my money back.* "Keep it," he shouted over his shoulder. He increased the pace of his walk and reached the fountain as the flower girl entered the square.

"Cyrus!" she called out to him again, and picked up the long length of her dress as she ran across the square toward him.

Niamh turned to him, befuddlement written on her face. "She seems to want to speak with you; should I wait?"

"No," he replied. "Take us out of here. Now."

The winds of the druid's teleport spell kicked up around them, stirring the dust at his feet. The flower girl was running, but she stopped as she saw the magic begin to take hold. She stood ten feet away, her cheeks glittering, tears tracing down her lovely dark skin from those green eyes that sparkled. She held out her hand with the coins in it and for the first time he saw the ring on her finger. Emerald, magnificent, a piece of jewelry worthy of a princess, not a flower girl.

Imina, he thought as the magics spun the winds around him, creating a wall of air between him and the crying flower girl that had seemed so familiar for some reason. *I forgot your face.* He stared at her, trying to burn it into his memory, but the teleport spell carried him away, back to Sanctuary, back to his guild and his life, and away from her once more.

THE LAST MOMENTS OF THE GEZHVET

Note: Takes place at the end of Chapter 12 of **Defender: The Sanctuary Series, Volume One**.

"Your poor dwarven friend, left to die alone ... he was alive, you recall, when they took him ... how do you think he died? Do you think it was painful? Do you think he kept his courage to the end? Or do you think he screamed and begged for mercy that would never be shown?" A twinkle lit the eye of the Gatekeeper, coupled with a smile that could only be described as sadistic. "Because I know."
　　　　　　　　—The Gatekeeper to Cyrus Davidon
　　　　　　　Avenger: The Sanctuary Series, Volume Two

He was bleeding as they carried him off, the monstrous horror of the massacre going on around him tempered by the agony of a thousand claws stabbing through the flaws in his armor. The points of them pierced the metal chainmail that was his last line of defense, cutting into him like knives ripping through his flesh. "Let me down, you grubby, sunlight-dwelling greenskin sons of whores!" A claw cut into his cheek and he tasted blood running down his tongue and through his mouth as he was carried over the cobbled stone of Enterra's throne room on the shoulders of goblins beyond numbering.

There were hundreds of them, half a thousand, perhaps, but it might as well have been a million. Narstron could feel his strength failing, the blood loss making his head swim as they carried him into a passage at the side of the throne room. As he passed over the threshold, he caught one last glimpse of Cyrus, his best friend. The warrior in black armor was fighting with his back to a stone wall, his sword cutting swaths of destruction through the goblin army.

The musty smell of the caves was heavy in the air as Narston lost sight of his friend. The natural wonder of being this deep in Rotan's holy ground was tempered not only by his fear but by the artificial construct of stones being placed into square halls and tunnels. He had always hoped to die deep below the earth but not here, where Rotan's holy ground had been desecrated by the cold, unnatural goblin architecture. Narston was aware of the cold air, but he barely felt it amidst the wounds, the cuts, the thousand searing hurts that enveloped him.

Narstron slammed his left hand down with all his remaining strength and saw it land hard on one of the goblins who was carrying him. The goblin, a scaled, green-skinned, snaggle-toothed beast, fell out of his line of sight, below the procession. But the rest of the goblins, however many of them there were, still had him up on their shoulders. They formed a crowd that was too large for him to resist, to fight back against. His right hand was numb from where their claws were still buried in it, immobilizing it. He felt his sword jarred from his fingers. He tried to roll, to fall off the shoulders of those who carried him, but he couldn't work free of the hands that gripped him, of the claws that bit into the flesh of his back and sides.

Narstron slapped out at another goblin, and this time he knew he broke something, perhaps a nose. The goblin staggered and fell below the tide of green-skinned foes that carried him on. *I hope he was trampled to death, crushed underfoot by this horde, this reckless mob.* The chanting was the worst, the voices of the goblins echoing through the cave as they went. "Gezhvet! Gezhvet!" they called as though trying to shout it into the depths of the earth so that Rotan himself could hear it. Narstron whipped a hand around again, this time missing anything, and he felt a sharp stab in his side for his troubles. He didn't scream, though, and he wouldn't; he refused to give this lot the satisfaction.

The block and mortar hallway widened ahead just before they burst out into a massive chamber, a room that looked like a theater he had once seen in Reikonos. It had room for standing parted by an aisle down the middle, leading up to a stage for the performance. *Except I doubt I'll enjoy the final act of this one.* It was dark, like home—like Fertiss, the dwarven capital—but his eyes had long since adjusted to that, the small torches burning in the corners of the room shedding enough light for him to see by. *Not nearly so much as I've been accustomed to living among the humans, though.*

He was carried down toward the stage, making one last attempt at resistance against the mob with his good hand. His blow landed home on a goblin's face and he snagged his gauntlet on a pointed green ear as he pulled it back. He heard the howl of pain and ripped as hard as he could, the lobstered metal joint still caught on the fragile ear. He heard a screech as it tore loose, taking the ear with it. His grin of satisfaction lasted all of five seconds before he was dumped unceremoniously against the surface of an upended surface. He hit hard enough that the wind was knocked out of him, but his legs caught him and kept him standing. Goblin claws seized hold of his left hand and yanked his gauntlet, ripping it free while others tugged free the right. He saw a green ear spiral to the floor where it was trod over, lost in a shuffle of green flesh.

Narstron felt himself gasp as a goblin, taller than the rest of them yet shorter than himself, reached out with a dagger and stabbed him through his left hand, driving it into the surface of the table behind him. Over the pain he could feel the grain of the wood against his hand, an odd sensation that was marred by the blistering pain in his palm. It took a moment for his shock-addled mind to realize it was the Emperor of Enterra himself, Y'rakh, who had done it to him. *Damn, that was the good hand. I can still kick them, at least—*

But he couldn't. The wave of goblins receded, save for Y'rakh, leering at him with yellow eyes as he moved to Narstron's other side. The dwarf felt himself slumping, using the hard wood surface he was butted up against for strength as he tried to remain standing. It was a fight against his legs, strength fading. He had his numb right hand at the ready to throw up if the Emperor came at him, but the agony from the knife thrust through his left hand on top of all his other injuries had left him exhausted. He could feel his legs crying out for permission to buckle. He looked down to see his armor red with blood. His own or that of his foes, he couldn't be sure. *Only going to get one shot at this ...*

Y'rakh came at him again, producing another knife from his belt. Narstron feinted as best he could, acting like he was going to block the knife with a bracer, but instead he changed direction at the last moment, jutting a finger at the goblin's eye as he came close. *The Cyrus Davidon strategy.* Narstron thought of his friend, surely dead now, with a trace of sorrow. He rammed his finger hard ahead, and it struck the bony skull of the goblin as Y'rakh turned to the side abruptly.

Narstron heard rather than felt his finger break through the numbness. His hand weakened and Y'rakh grasped it, ramming it back against the wood surface behind Narstron. He felt the long, thin blade of the dagger cut into his open palm. He could feel the resistance for a fraction of a second as the tip of the knife ripped through the flesh and encountered tendon and bone, but that lasted only a moment and it was through, the numbness gone and his hand blazing with fire as it, too, was pinned to the table.

Narstron kicked out with his right leg with everything he had—pain, rage, more than a little fear—and he caught the Emperor of the goblins squarely in his tapered midsection, just below his bony ribs. The breath rushed out of the goblin's mouth, filling the air in front of Narstron with a squalid stink of bad meat.

They killed Cyrus and Andren. Killed them both. "I'll make you pay!" Narstron's shout echoed as he lanced out again, catching the Emperor of Enterra with a metal boot in the head that caused him to fall backward, nearly off the slightly raised stage upon which they both stood.

The click of a thousand claws touching the stone floors beneath the dais was an eerie sound. All the goblins were quiet and tense, looking as though they wanted to move forward in a mass and eat him alive to avenge their Emperor's injury. *Let them come. I'll kick until I can't kick anymore, rip my damned hands off if need be, slam my shoulders, pauldron-first, into their slimy mouths, break their teeth—*

"My friends," came a calm voice from the back of the chamber. Amusement wafted from a black-cloaked figure who had his hood pulled back, revealing a dark elf's features, gaunt to the point of looking almost like the bones of a skull, only a thin layer of skin stretched over them. "There is no need to be so harsh; his fight is over."

Heavy, guttural growls came from Emperor Y'rakh as he spoke in his own language, in what sounded to Narstron's ears like bitter cursing. "This dwarf is as fearsome as our legends say," he spoke, now back in the human language, not averting his eyes from Narstron but raising his voice so it carried over the chamber. "It is as you told us: he is surely the Gezhvet."

"Would I have lied to you?" The dark elf's smile was as thin as the rest of him and more than a little overly satisfied.

"The price you demanded was high." Emperor Y'rakh said looking over his shoulder at Narstron. *I'd carve him open if I had my sword. If I could bite him, I would sink my teeth into his throat. For Cyrus. For Andren.*

"The price is always high when the reward is so very rich," the dark elf said, making his way through the neat rows of goblins lining the room. "Is saving your life and your empire not worth a trifling sacrifice?" The dark elf brandished a hammer, a metal object with intricate detail. It had an obsidian oblong head that looked more impressive than anything he'd seen from the blacksmiths of Fertiss. The dark elf paused just past the throng, at the base of the stage, staring up at Narstron with an innocent, almost curious expression. "So ... what will you do now? Now that you have your Gezhvet in hand?"

Y'rakh looked back at him, and Narstron felt the creep of something dark in the goblin's vacant expression as it turned colder. He felt the hatred seep into it. *He hates me. Truly hates me. This is no simple invasion being turned back. There's something else at play here, something I'm not getting.* "Now," the goblin said in a quiet, hissing voice, "we tear him to pieces and render his prophecy moot."

"Moot is such a lovely word," the dark elf said smoothly, holding the hammer daintily in one hand as though it were weightless, while running his thin fingers over his black robe with the other. "If I may suggest, though, something you might not have considered, with these adventurers—humans, dwarves and such—death is hardly certain. I could ... ensure that he never rose again, if you'd like." The dark elf grinned. "I can solve this problem for you more surely and definitely than simply tearing him to pieces."

Narstron watched, the pain in his hands from the blades jutting out of them keeping him from saying more. *Are they really arguing about how best to kill me? Who did I so grievously offend? I bet it was that elven witch, Vara.*

"I don't know about that, Malpravus," the Emperor said. "Tearing a body to pieces tends to solve most of your problems with it." There was a wary air about the goblin. "What price would you charge for this service you offer?"

"You would think so ill of me as to assume I would come to you with this offer solely to enrich myself?" There was a hint of reproach in the dark elf's voice, but Narstron could hear a lack of sincerity in his tone. *I wonder if the goblins hear it as well?* "Allow me to do this, then," Malpravus said, "in the name of our continued friendship and goodwill. Allow me to end this threat that has hung over you for so long. Definitively."

The thinly slitted eyes of the goblin watched the dark elf, giving his words careful consideration. When the nod of assent came, Narstron almost missed it, it was so subtle. The Emperor stepped aside with measured movements, relegating himself to the front rank of the goblins as though ready to charge the dais should something go awry.

Malpravus climbed to the place where Narstron was fixed, hands still struck through, anchoring him to the upturned table. "Dear boy, I expect you've had better days." The dark elf looked him over with an appraising eye, as though about to sell him off in the slave markets of Gren. "Indeed, you look as though you put up a impressive fight before they brought you low. I trust all that defiance has run its natural course?"

"Get on with it if you're going to get on with it," Narstron said, trying to keep from babbling. His hands were cold and aching now, the warmth of the blood that had been running down them long since faded. Now a chill was setting in, the frigid underground caves getting to him at last.

"Oh, I shall," the dark elf said with a grin, and there was a thunking noise as he set the hammer down on the floor next to his feet. "But first I'm simply trying to get the measure of you. I don't recall seeing you with Sanctuary before." He squinted his eyes. "You must be new."

"I'm feeling a bit old at the moment," Narstron said, hearing his words slur. "A bit worn through."

"I suppose you would," Malpravus said, steepling his fingers before stretching his knuckles. The fingers were long and slender, like the branches of a gnarled old tree made bare by winter's edge. He manipulated them digit by digit, the cracking of his pronounced knuckles sounding like dry tinder being broken. "Your friends are dead, your guild is almost entirely wiped out—" Narstron caught a toothy grin from Malpravus on this point—"It's been a hard day, to say the least, and I suppose it's not about to get much easier for you." One of his hands disappeared into his sleeve and returned a moment later with a little flourish. A red gemstone was pinched between his thumb and forefinger, a ruby that hardly glistened at all, especially in the dull light of the cave.

"If this is a marriage proposal, I'm afraid I'm going to have to beg off," Narstron said, staring at the dark gem. "Not the least of which reason is that you're not my type." He tugged on his arms, felt the pain in his palms.

"Also, I can't feel my hands."

"You'll feel nothing, soon enough," Malpravus said, smile widening. "Tell me, though, before you go—was Alaric with you tonight?"

"What?" Narstron watched the dark elf, the goblins behind him fading into the background as if they were being absorbed into the cave itself. He felt his legs grow weaker. *Not sure I should answer that.* "No."

"A pity," Malpravus said, and his expression grew more clouded. "It would have wrapped things up a bit too neatly if he was, I suppose. There is some logical limit to the number of birds you can kill with one well-thrown stone, after all."

A little connection was bridged in Narstron's mind, some dying light igniting like a lamp catching the flame. "You did this. All of this. Brought them down on us, when they shouldn't have known we were coming?"

"I did," Malpravus said. "I must confess, it was one of my cleverer maneuvers, being able to hand these fine allies the Gezhvet," he gestured at Narstron and there was a groundswell of goblin noise from the haze behind him, "and also procure something I wanted in the process." He nudged the hammer with a foot, and Narstron's eyes fell on it, his question of what a Gezhvet was forgotten for the moment.

"Is that ..." Narstron let his head drift downward, "is that Terrenus?"

Malpravus looked down. "The Hammer of Rotan? Indeed." The skeletal smile was back.

Narstron felt the cold calculation run over him. "You killed Cyrus. You killed Andren." *This is going to hurt. But who cares?*

"In point of fact, I didn't kill anyone." Malpravus's cold eyes still held a gleam of satisfaction.

Narstron felt the slow sliding as he worked his arms forward, felt the fiery edge of the blades carve through his hands as he put every last bit of his strength into working them forward. "You brought this on us. On all of us."

Malpravus brought his hands up, as though he were about to cast a spell. "Oh, *that*. Well, yes, I suppose I did." He grinned, gleeful. "I have always known which direction to fan the flames of power, after all." He paused and closed his eyes. "Now, if you'll excuse me, dear boy, I have your end to attend to.

"Oh, of course," Narstron said. "Don't mind me." *Cyrus. Andren.* He felt the tug of resistance on his hands and kept his eyes anchored on

Malpravus, only feet away from him. He leaned forward slowly, feeling the blades rip at him, but kept from crying out. The pain was duller than it had been when the knives first went in—duller, but by no means gone. *Sweet Rotan, the agony!* He gritted his teeth together but kept his expression flat, trying not to give a hint. *If I can get the hammer —if that's really Rotan's hammer—I can break through them, carve the Emperor's head in like he's a carnival bell needing to be rung, drag Cyrus and Andren to the exit, find a healer and a resurrection spell—*

Malpravus's eyes were still closed, but his hands glowed now, a black sort of luminescence. It was like lightning behind the darkest thundercloud, a hint of brightness escaping a shroud, and the dark elf's lips moved in time with some magic that he wove. The red ruby was still clenched in his fingers.

Knock him asunder, Narstron thought. *Pull free, grab the hammer ... make ... them ... PAY—*

His hands ripped free of the blades pinning him to the upturned table and he roared, a full-throated cry of battle like nothing he'd ever given off before. *Like Cyrus.* The goblins were there again, out of the background. They stood out in stark clarity, green figures against the dark cave walls, shuffling back from the sheer ferocity of his warcry. Narstron's legs held and he forced all his strength into them, willing them to hold his weight even though he felt so heavy. The sorcerer in front of him was only a step away, and he reached for the hammer, clumsily—

All the breath seeped out of him in the next instant as the darkness swept forward from Malpravus's hands and wrapped around him. A succession of lights flashed before his eyes like a blanket being dragged quickly on and off of him on a bright summer's day. Narstron saw the moments of his life—the day he left Fertiss, the face of the maid in Reikonos who'd given him his first time, the dark, homey guildhall of the Kings—

The day he'd met Cyrus in the Pelar Hills, sword in hand. *There is no finer warrior. There is no fear in him.* Narstron's teeth ground together and he clenched his hand around the hammer's handle. *There* was *no fear in him. I should be afraid now, shouldn't I?* A grim smile formed on his lips. *Maybe I did learn something in all our conversations about the God of War, after all. I'm committed to it now. My purpose is decided. One last gasp of defiance at this bastard who killed my friends—*

His fingers gripped the heft of the hammer, and he felt warmth surge through him, one that faded quickly with the last flash. *Cyrus would defy. Cyrus would defy to the last.* He lifted it, felt it come up with ease, even as his legs failed him and his knees hit the hard rock floor of the cave. His shoulder landed and there was a clink of metal against the stone. Unyielding. His weight fell on it as his body unbalanced and all the strength began to leave him, a slow, seeping feeling as the last warmth began to drain from him.

A face appeared as he slumped, his body oozing beneath him like water poured out of the tankard that gave it shape and purpose. The dark blue skin was stretched just enough to cover the skull beneath, but not enough to hide the grin. "A valiant effort, my friend," Malpravus said with a ghastly smile. "But as I said, your fight is done. You have only moments remaining. Seconds left, enough for last words and little else before your life, your soul, departs you forever." He held up the ruby again, in front of Narstron's eyes, and there was a glimmer in it now, at the center. "So...what say you?"

Narstron looked up at the hollow, sunken sockets and the barely-there eyes behind them, devoid of anything but some sallow glee at the spectacle they were witnessing. *Only one thing to say to that, really.* He moved a hand, beckoning Malpravus closer. He opened his lips just slightly, so he could speak, and the dark elf leaned in.

Narstron felt the tangy blood still in his mouth from earlier, from the pummeling he'd taken at the hands of the goblins. What little saliva he had left he gathered with the blood and the breath that he felt crying to come out of him.

He spit it out in one last gasp, one final, furious burst of defiance, and saw it hit the dark elf's navy face and run down, the amusement and glee that had been there only a moment earlier vanishing into hard lines and anger.

"My fight's not over," Narstron said with the last, unhurried breath, and his eyes alighted on the ruby once more. It glistened, glowed brighter, and he felt the last of himself flee his body, leaving the pain behind, as the bright red gem glowed with a light of its own while his faded for the last time.

"So do I," Cyrus said with a calm realization. He could see Narstron's face in his mind's eye, the last image of him being dragged off by the hands of a hundred goblins. "He lived like a warrior. He died like a warrior. And everything else you have to say is lies."

—Cyrus Davidon to The Gatekeeper
Avenger: The Sanctuary Series, Volume Two

THE GREENEST FIELDS

Note: Takes place immediately following the final chapters of **Crusader: The Sanctuary Series, Volume Four**.

One

It was a simple trail of blood like a thousand she'd seen, little spots of red amongst the fallen green leaves. It led off across the plains toward the edge of the Waking Woods. There were shadows around them, a darkness creeping in as twilight came. She sniffed and caught the smell of the one who'd passed this way only an hour or so earlier, his strong, wretched scent still clinging to the weeds like death clings to a corpse. *And he smells like death,* Martaina Proelius thought to herself, *like a wielder of it, like a carrier of it, like a man who brings it with him everywhere he goes.*

She was tall, even for an elf, and her legs were longer than most. There were others with her, at her back, the smell of their horses strong in the air. There were two men immediately behind her and a host just a little further back, almost a hundred men ahorse. She had them back a short distance so they didn't interfere with her sense of smell, her sense of taste. She picked up a leaf fallen into the mud and placed it in her mouth, just for a moment, savoring it. She felt the tang of the greenery, but more than that was the dirt, the blood, and the scent of both was heavy upon it. "Not far," she announced, speaking around the leaf but nearly in a whisper, and heard her words relayed in a shout to the men behind her, the host, the ones following. It reminded her curiously of a time she'd seen humans turn loose dogs to do the very same work she was doing now, a whole pack of them.

But in her case, the pack was following, keeping the sound of their chatter and the stamping of the horses' feet on the muddy ground far, far back from her. From her work.

She spat out the leaf, and her long legs carried her onward again, her cloak trailing like a dog in her wake. She was running, and she heard the men spurred to action behind her, the horses coming to a gallop to try and close the distance. It was a hunting party, a war party of Sanctuary.

Except it wasn't. The men were new, not truly of Sanctuary, not most of them, anyway. They were men of Luukessia, tired and bloodthirsty, with anger boiling over from the loss of their land and ready for a savage kill. She ran along, cold. There was enough hot blood behind her; no need to add her own to the mix.

She carried her bow, the arrow nocked on the string, running the way her father had taught her—with care, always with care. Her sharp eyes took in the crags, rocks and uneven ground in the low light of the woefully small moon. It was enough for her to be going by, though she dared not look back, not at the men behind her, not at their torches. For more than one reason.

"How far would you say?" One of them spoke behind her, and she didn't look back at him, just kept going. She could have answered; she planned to but waited. She could hear the clack of his armor, the puff of his breaths coming as he wheezed, just a little, catching up to her. The horses were at a canter now, keeping their pace far behind her, the distance between them now more than a hundred feet, closer to a hundred and fifty. That worked well for her, she liked it. The two men immediately behind her, on the other hand, they were close. Too close. For comfort, anyway. The one started to speak again. "I said—"

"I heard you," she said quietly, finally slowing to a walk. When she moved on the hunt, it was always in a darting, fast motion. Motion was one of the quickest ways for prey to give themselves away; motion, shadow, the outline, the sound, the discrepancy with the background color. If you were going to move, best to do it quickly; you were already making noise and motion anyway. She took a quick sniff. "Less than a mile ahead."

"You're sure it's him?" The voice was quiet, not disappointed, exactly, but not thrilled, either. Mostly winded, that much was obvious. She knew the voice, knew it better than she knew any other. In the last year and a half, oddly, she hadn't really missed it.

"Yes, Thad," she said, listening to her husband's metal boots drown out the sounds of the forest ahead, the Waking Woods, as he crunched leaves underfoot. "His stride is distinct from the others, his plate boots are unique, he's leaving a blood trail, exactly the same as the one we found in the wreckage of the tent—"

"Okay," Thad puffed again. "I just figured, with a battlefield like the one we just came from, there might be room for error—"

"There is not," she said. "Not for this. Not for blood. It's distinct. If it was a footprint alone, maybe." She drew up to her full height and finally turned, the light of the torches spoiling her night vision as she made a calculated decision to look him in the eye. "It's him. This man escaped from the dark elven command tent."

"That likely makes him a general," Samwen Longwell said, lingering just past Thad. Martaina gave him a cool look, trying not to give anything away. Longwell, for his part, blushed briefly. "Or an adjutant, an aide—something of that sort. Someone we'd rather not allow to get back to Saekaj."

Martaina felt a searing heat in her cheeks, felt the cool night air blow over them, highlighting the warmth even further. "I won't allow him to get away, though time spent in discussion does not aid my tracking."

"Right," Thad said, looking slightly chastened. He almost seemed to draw back slightly, as though he'd done some wrong. *But then, he's always been like that.* "Carry on, then."

She exchanged a brief look with Longwell, which seemed to say much the same, with perhaps a little additional meaning that she didn't dare untangle right then and there. Martaina turned away from the men, back to the track. She let out a long, slow breath as she picked up her pace, running across crunching leaves, trying to focus entirely on the task at hand—indeed, as she always did in times of great strife.

Two

One Thousand Years Earlier

Martaina rolled off of him, satiated, her breaths coming in long gasps while his came quicker, more winded. She pulled her naked body free of his, rolling off the fine bed that she'd slept in the night before, something of a rarity for her—though it was becoming more common nowadays—and began to dress herself, starting with the worn, dirty animal skin breeches that came first in her ensemble.

"You always have this boundless energy," Nethan said, still trying to regain his breath. She could feel his eyes watching her bare backside as she slid the grungy pants on, shimmying into them. "I'm a planter and I'm not half as athletic as you are."

"You own a plantation," Martaina said somewhat dryly, not letting her smile show as she tied the rope belt that kept her breeches on. Finishing that, she sat on the edge of the bed to pull on the worn leather boots that she'd skinned herself, "I don't think that's the same as being in a field, pushing a plow all day long the way your servants do."

"Quite right," Nethan said, chortling. She could sense his gaze shift away now that all she had to offer was a view of her unclothed back. She pondered for a moment why she didn't face him while dressing then pushed the thought aside when the first answer that came her way was shame. "It's not such a bad life, sitting upon the porch overseeing things."

"Indeed," Martaina agreed, sliding her loose, deer-hide shirt over her torso and turning to face him before lacing it up with the string she'd spent hours making one day. All her clothes were self-made. She cast a glance over at Nethan's attire, lying on the floor where they'd fallen the night before. Silk shirts, cloth jackets, other assorted finery along with jewelry rested on the dresser. Looking it over, she felt a brief entwining of envy and hope. *To have such things—perhaps someday. Someday soon.* "It's really lovely work if you can get it, being a noble son of a landed plantation owner." She let her smile crook. "If only I could find a way to do such a thing myself."

"Eh?" Nethan said, and looked sidelong at her. "So, where are you off to today?"

"Hunting," Martaina said, sliding her cloak on. It was without doubt the nicest thing she had, made from cloth that had fallen out of a caravan wagon and into the mud. She'd watched it jealously, keeping her eyes on the wagon until it was out of sight and sure not to return for a stray bolt of cloth that had gone errantly into a mud puddle. She'd hardly believed that the overseer walking next to the wagon would let such a thing escape as she'd cradled it in her arms and run back to her father with it. Her mind returned to the room she was in, on the Vierest Plantation twenty miles outside Pharesia. The curtains flapped in the slight breeze as she stared down at Nethan, her lover of three months, lingering beneath the sheets as though he had no intention of rousting himself now.

She leaned down, letting her bare flesh rub against the inside of her animal skin tunic as she lay across the sheets, drawing a nearly scandalized look from Nethan as her dirty furs brushed his white satin. He said nothing, though, looking up to her and forcing a smile. "What about you?" she asked, smiling.

"I'll need to take a gander at the fields by noon," Nethan said and then yawned. "Until then, I expect I'll sleep a bit longer." He patted the bed. "Why don't you undress and join me; surely your hunting can wait?"

"It's after sun up," Martaina said and pulled away, feeling the stir of regret. "Unless I'm very fortunate, I won't be getting breakfast this morning because I didn't start early enough—"

"Have something in the kitchen before you go," Nethan said, waving his hand toward the door. "The house servants prepare plenty for the field hands, they can surely spare some bread for you, maybe some pottage. Tell them I said so." He yawned again. "Still and all, I think you should stay." His eyes drifted shut. "Until a civilized hour, at least."

"Your idea of a civilized hour is far later than mine," she said, watching him wistfully, stroking her brown hair back behind her ears. It was hanging loose and wild this morning. It was never much tamed, but she kept it in a tight knot most of the time. She'd let it free last night while she'd been seducing him, but now it would take time to re-knot.

"It a kinder hour than this one," he said, opening one eye, "and it would allow us to rise in leisure, go down to the kitchens to eat the breakfast that the servants normally prepare for me—"

"Which I would guess is not pottage and bread," she said with a little irony.

"And come back up here for additional ... leisure time," he grinned beneath his closed eyes and pawed at her, grasping at her breast. His hand cupped her, not terribly gently but not painfully, either, so she let it rest there, very nearly rolling her eyes.

"If past experience is any guide, I doubt very much you have another bout of leisure in you today," Martaina said and slowly stood, letting his hand fall back to the bed. After the first moment, when his grip had loosened, it had actually felt good. "Perhaps tomorrow night I'll see you again."

"Indeed," Nethan said, opening an eye to look at her again, his smile solid and genuine. "I shall look forward to the hour when we meet once more."

"Yes," said Martaina, feeling none of his sincerity and all the discomfort of a woman terribly out of place. "I shall look forward to it as well." She leaned down and kissed him, felt his lips return the pressure just slightly, then walked out the door as she knotted the cloak around her neck.

The walls of the hallway outside were neither painted nor bare wood but covered in a texture that Nethan had called "wallpaper" when she'd asked him. With the embossments on it, it didn't feel much like paper; it felt like someone had embroidered cloth and covered entire walls with it. She took care but ran her fingers down it, feeling the raised bumps along the thick callouses on the pads of her fingers. *To live in such a place, with such fine things,* she thought.

She walked down the staircase at the far end of the hall—the one at the back of the house that let out in the kitchens, not the impressively carpeted one that looked out over a balcony into a grand foyer—and took every step lightly, so quietly that she couldn't even hear herself move over the noise from the kitchens below.

She took one look around at the roaring ovens and the servants who eyed her with knowing smiles and hushed whispers. and brushed out the back door next to the stairs without a word, leaving behind the heavy, doughy smell in the air that masked the scent of herself—the scent of guilt that had settled on her along with the sheen of sweat that still covered her skin.

Three

Martaina slipped back under the heavy canopy of the Iliarad'ouran Woods a short time later after traversing the wide fields around Nethan's plantation at a run. She wasn't even close to being out of breath by the time she reached the far edge of the field, feeling the shade of the leaves on the massive trees block the sun from her face as she quickened her pace. The woods were home, and the camp was not far away. Had been for weeks. The available land of the Iliarad'ouran was shrinking by the year, a slow, inevitable tightening of their bounds.

Martaina tried not to think of that as she ran along, making little noise as she jumped over tree trunks, dodged roots and slipped around the trunks of the enormous trees. The smell of greenery was thick in the air, the fresh morning scent of the Iliarad'ouran Woods. She caught a whiff of something and paused before running up the root of a tree that extended some five hundred feet into the air above her. She edged along the side of the trunk, the patches of rough bark caressing her hand as she pulled her bow off her shoulder and nocked an arrow, all without having actually seen an animal yet.

She took another sniff, more quietly this time, and she smelled it again. A deer. She eased around the trunk, letting one eye slip out from behind cover first. Her quarry was there, unaware, the deer quartered away from her. It was a fat doe, big bodied and wild, like she'd come to expect here in the Iliarad'ouran Woods. And why should it not be? They were plentiful, hunted only by her people and the occasional group from Pharesia at the King's behest. Planters were commanded to leave them be, even though they were a nuisance to the crops.

Martaina eased out further, preparing her shot. She was so quiet that there was nary a sound for her prey to be aware of, and the animal kept eating, the light fal'thes grass that grew in a patch where the canopy was broken overhead making only the slightest ruffle as the doe disturbed it. *This is a chance to redeem myself for my late start.* Plentiful though they were, the deer of the Iliarad'ouran Woods were still canny, cagey creatures that kept perpetually on the run, and catching one upwind was still a pleasant surprise, especially this early in the day.

She felt the tension of the string as she drew back her bow. She made shots like this every day, both in practice and against an animal of some kind, though not always such a ripe one as this. She let her other eye slide out from behind the tree trunk, now gauging her distance to the target, and raised the bow just slightly to compensate. She aimed behind the shoulder, the big broadhead tip on the arrow designed to tear through meat and keep the animal from escaping too far. That was bad for both her and the animal; a slow, painful death for it and the chance of escape to somewhere she might not be able to retrieve it. Both concerns were pressing, but as her stomach rumbled she knew which concerned her more.

The arrow flew through the air with a sharp whistle, and she watched it sail a little forward into the front right shoulder of the doe. The reaction was immediate: the doe bolted but her injured leg failed, causing the animal to stumble. Martaina followed the arrow with another, but this one she fumbled slightly in her excitement. It went high and through the top of the back as she grimaced. *The tenderloin,* she thought, *I just shredded it. Father will not be pleased.* The arrow stuck out of its back and the doe fell to the ground, then flopped in the long grass, legs flailing in the air as the animal bucked once, twice, then lay still.

Martaina kept her distance and listened again to the rumble in her stomach. She knew even with the animal at hand she was still hours from being able to eat, hours of preparation and cooking. With a sigh, letting out the tension that had been been building within her since she'd left Nethan behind, she eased forward toward the carcass, pulling her knife as she did so. She didn't really want to drag the entire weight of the creature back to the camp, so she set about the business of leaving the heavy, useless parts behind. She opened up the deer along the belly, the smell being something she'd never become used to. She blanched at the stink of feces and half-digested grass. She held her sleeve up to her nose with one hand as she made selective cuts with the other, then reached in with both and dragged the guts and stomach out, leaving them on the ground. She tied a quick sling with little bit of rope she had in her pack and began to drag the doe across the uneven ground.

Her legs burned with the effort as she pulled the animal through the woods, sticking to the trail she'd begun to make over the last few months, the straight line between camp and the plantation. She would have sworn she never followed it exactly, but looking at the foliage, she realized there was a clear pattern, that she had left all the signs to give anyone interested in tracking her a very visible reminder of where she spent her nights when she wasn't in camp. *Not that anyone cares.* She reconsidered that. *Not that anyone cares enough to mention it.*

She crested a low rise, straining under the weight of the animal she was dragging. She could feel the beads of sweat popping out on her forehead, settling over the layer that she'd already accumulated in the evening and the first thing in the morning. This was the sweat of labor, though, not of simple, pleasurable gyration. Her muscles were accustomed to fast, lithe movement that came from carrying her lean frame from place to place. Dragging animals alone was not something she usually did, not over distances such as this. Not when there were animals closer to camp that didn't require such intensive labor. Still, the doe was a good prize, and it had practically wandered into her path. It would feed them for some time, and some of the pieces would be useful for other endeavors.

There was noise over the last crest as she came to the top of a small hill, and she knew the camp was not far. It was usually a quiet place, with only the three of them now. Unless there was—

Martaina dropped her burden, let the rope roll right off her shoulder, and pounded her feet against the worn-down trail that she'd made over the last months, going into a full-out run down the slight hollow ahead of her and then up again to find herself just outside camp. She jumped up onto an exposed root that stood three feet above the ground and grasped her bow, holding off on nocking an arrow as she let her eyes watch the scene before her unfold.

"It's the King's land," the guardsman said—she'd met him before, his name was Hesshan—looking at her father while waving a finger in the older man's face.

"The woodsmen have had the right of hunting on these lands for generations," Martaina's father—she thought of him less as father and more by his name, Amalys—replied, his long, bedraggled beard hiding his utter lack of interest in the conversation, "since long before there was a bloody King, a Kingdom, or any of the other things you've got carved upon that breast of yours so you can beat them with pride every night." He gestured at the boiled leather cuirass that the guardsman wore, metal etchings placed around the breastplate of it denoting his unit insignia.

"Your right of hunting was never guaranteed by any document or proclamation that King Danay has ever made," the guardsman said smugly. Still, his hand went unconsciously to his armor, stroking the etchings with his chainmail glove.

"Well, why don't you have your King come out here and tell me how I'm stealing his game?" Amalys looked at the guardsman with barely disguised disinterest, his hand falling to his big belly and rubbing it like he had an itch right around the middle of it.

"The King has better things to do than deal with poaching, layabout scum," Hesshan said, his winged helm catching a reflected light. He had three compatriots with him, all of them shuffling behind him.

"Now I'm scum, am I?" Amalys's ire was barely visible as he stared at the guardsman, but Martaina could see it there. "For living off the lands the way my ancestors did? For refusing to become a servant or a cultivator on a farm, bowing to your King's dictates to produce so he can take half of the grain I harvest? Half the herds I raise?" Amalys spat on the ground between them, the shadow of the canopy above breaking long enough to cast him in a beam of light. "I'll take my living from the forest as I always have, thank you very much. Subject to no man, and no man subject to me."

"You are subject to the King," Hesshan said grimly, with an aura of menace. Now his hand danced closer to the blade at his belt, lingering close to the hilt. Martaina coughed, clearing her throat, and the guardsmen, Hesshan and his three compatriots looked up all at once. Her arrow was now nocked and aimed at Hesshan's head. She was ready to shoot him as she had the doe. He'd probably die faster, though. With a stir of surprise, she realized she was pointing her bow at a living elf, a person, and she felt a subtle tremor run through her hand that she tried to conceal from sight.

"It's against the laws to threaten a guardsman of the Kingdom," Hesshan said, his ruddy face flushing with anger. His hand still hovered near the hilt of his sword.

"I'm not threatening you," Martaina said in a clear voice. "I'm aiming at the raccoon behind you."

Hesshan shuffled, uncertain, then looked back for just a moment. "I don't see any raccoon."

"With your city eyes always so focused on kissing the arse of your immediate superior, I'm surprised you can see anything farther away than a hands-length," Martaina said coolly, drawing a snicker from Amalys. She didn't know for a fact that the guardsman spent any time kissing up to his superior, but she'd heard Nethan say as much happened constantly in Pharesia, that it was just a fact of the bureaucracy, and the only way to ever advance was by currying favor.

"I see the raccoon," another voice boomed out on the clearing, high and loud, drawing the attention of the guardsmen. Gareth appeared from just behind a fallen log of a smaller tree, only a couple feet in diameter. Martaina smiled as he appeared, and he shot her a reckless grin from behind his own bow, arrow ready to fly. "It seems to follow this one around," he gestured at Hesshan, "incessantly, as though he smells particularly fascinating." He squinted. "Hmm. You know what? Upon further examination, I believe that may in fact be a skunk, likely attracted by the smell of this one's hindquarters."

Martaina found that didn't merit much more than a small chuckle, but Hesshan flushed. "You think you can threaten us, you Iliarad'ouran freeloaders? You leeches, cozied up to the skin of whatever beast you can find to draw blood from?"

"And thus we reach the end of your knowledge about the natural world," Gareth wisecracked, still looking down the shaft of the arrow he had leveled at the guardsmen. Being older, he had far more skill with his bow than Martaina and could shoot faster even than she. "Perhaps for your next analogy you could compare us to something you're more familiar with – like the bakers who make bread in your city."

"You leeches couldn't afford bread in my city," Hesshan shot back, undaunted by the arrows gleaming in the low light of the forest eaves. "Your kind has no place in our Kingdom. You're the lowest of the low, the last vestiges of forest-dwelling savages of ages past. You're out of time, out of place, and your day is drawing to a close." He jerked his hand away from the hilt of his sword. "Kill us, they'll send more. Your pitch is narrowing, and the time's coming where you won't be allowed free lease of these lands anymore."

"You'll drag us out of these woods good and cold and dead," Amalys said. "We've been living here in the Iliarad'ouran all our lives, and the lives of our fathers, and all the generations past 'til those days no one can even remember. We'll take our meat fresh from the day's kill, our milk is the forest's stream, and our life is as large as we care to live it. No matter how much your Kingdom grows, no matter how pretty and civilized your lot becomes, eschewing the hard work of the hunt for the easy slaughter of a cow's haunch and goat's milk on the table in the hovel your King says your class is allowed to buy." Amalys cleared his throat and spat again, taking care to avoid Hesshan's boots. Martaina was certain she would not have afforded the arrogant guardsman the same courtesy. "Now get out of here before my impetuous youths let go of their arrows along with their good judgment."

Hesshan looked like he wanted to answer, but he didn't, instead shuffling slowly away, a few steps at a time, from Amalys, making no threatening moves but alternating his gaze from Gareth to Martaina in turn. "All right, then."

"And tell your King there are three of us here," Amalys said, almost spitting again. "If he can honestly discern how the three of us are impacting his bloody game stock in these woods, I'll move off the land myself and become one of his thrice-damned farmers." Amalys made a sound low in his throat. "As if King Danay has ever even set foot in these woods with a bow in his hands."

Hesshan said nothing more, and with a last spiteful look, he and his guardsmen shuffled off, back toward the path that Martaina knew was still up above the hill. She and Gareth watched them the whole way, never moving their arrows off target until they were out of sight.

"That skunk'll be back, you know," Gareth said, all trace of his confidence and recklessness gone, replaced by deep-etched lines of worry.

"He always does wander back," Amalys said, his face unburdened by this like it was as casual a proclamation as the weather turning sunny. "I suppose we should move our camp again, make it more difficult for him for a piece, until he wises up and sniffs us out again." He surveyed the area around him, the tents still pitched in the little flat space next to a brook. "Well, come on then," he said, and it was all command, "let's get our home moved up and gone."

Four

They packed up and moved within a quarter hour, their few possessions easily hauled off in a canvas sack apiece. Martaina let Gareth drag a sling specially designed for the deer as they trudged along, making their way west through the Iliarad'ouran Woods as the sun shone overhead, searching out the gaps between the boughs and leaves to shine down slivers of sunlight on the forest floor.

Gareth was a handsome enough fellow, Martaina had always thought. He'd been ever-present during her raising, though, and felt like a brother more than anything, though they were not related by blood. His brow was plainly troubled now and Martaina could see his countenance darken with every step they took from the last campsite. It was the third they'd chosen in the last few months, the wild, unchecked areas of the forest diminishing by the day as loggers and guards came to put the claim in for more and more land around Pharesia for the King.

"He knows," Gareth said under his breath as they followed behind Amalys a ways. Martaina's father made his way with a walking stick, an exaggerated limp hobbling his movement. She'd watched it disappear in camp, when he paid little attention to it, then saw it become more pronounced whenever it was mentioned. As a consequence, he carried the walking stick with him often, though he rarely leaned on it in practice outside of the camp. *Not that he got out of camp much anymore.* "About your nightly predations with the farmer," Gareth said.

"And that should concern me?" Martaina said, speaking low, matching Gareth's hushed whisper. She was well over the age of maturity, and the idea of her father worrying himself over her taking a lover should have been laughable. Still, she felt nervous tension at the thought. She hadn't done much to hide her affair, feeling almost rebellious about it. *So what if he knows? I'm plenty old enough, and still do all my work, my cleaning. It's my leisure time.*

"I don't know if it should concern you," Gareth said, eyeing her impassively. "That's between you and your father."

"He won't say anything if he hasn't already," she said, kicking up a pile of leaves as she passed through it, suddenly unconcerned about passing undisturbed. "Not that it's any of his business. We're still fed, and I still do my part." She felt a flush in her cheeks. "More than him, anyway." Gareth said nothing to this, the burden on his back forcing him to lean forward as he walked, like a gnarled tree tilting away from a furious wind. "You disagree?" she asked.

"I think it little concerns me," Gareth said. "But I thought you should be aware that he knows."

"Has he said anything to you?"

"Little enough," Gareth said, and his quicksilver smile appeared. "I believe he might have made mention of something as I came into camp this morning myself."

"Why, Gareth," Martaina said, suddenly unable to control a grin, "were you away all night as well?"

"I may have been," Gareth said, his lips pursed, insufferably pleased.

"Is this how a woodsman of the Iliarad'ouran comports himself?" she asked, still speaking in low tones, but her hushed voice was more than a little mocking. "Sneaking out in the hours of the night to meet a lover, probably sleeping in a soft bed instead of on the hard ground the way you were raised to, eating city food and being desirous of all the little material treasures that bind the city folk to their permanent hovels and unchained slavery?"

"You sound like your father," Gareth said with a smirk, "though it loses a bit of its luster without the conviction spread heavy on every word. Also, the fact that you spend your nights sweating under the loins of a farmer is a bit of a blow to your credibility on the subject."

"He's not much of a farmer," Martaina said. "More of a planter, really."

"Oh?" Gareth said, his smirk undimmed. "That means he merely watches while his lessers do the farming, doesn't it?"

She let her head bob as she felt heat unrelated to the shining sun beaming down on her head. "More or less."

"This will do," Amalys pronounced as they reached a low dip next to the creek they'd followed. By Martaina's guess they'd traversed something approaching seven miles, though it was hardly precise. She looked unconsciously to the east, trying to calculate how much additional time she'd have to spend walking to and from Nethan's plantation. She frowned.

It wasn't favorable.

"It would appear that both you and I are ill-considered in your father's plans," Gareth muttered under his breath.

"If he does indeed know," Martaina replied, equally quietly, "I'd say we were well-considered in his plans to move camp. After all, why make anything easier on us?"

"True enough," Gareth replied, "as we are the last of those who do the work around here." He shrugged the ropes off his shoulders, letting them fall to the earth as he stretched, pushing his arms to the sky as he squinted, as though he could somehow work the knots Martaina knew he was experiencing out of his muscles by simple stretching.

"Think about it," Martaina said, shifting back and forth on her long legs, "if we left to pursue other options, he might have to go out and do the hunting work for himself."

"He might indeed," Amalys rumbled as he turned back to them, causing Martaina to exchange a shocked, wide-eyed look with Gareth. "And you know what that would mean? Plumper animals, prompter breakfasts, not having to wait for you lot to come dragging in from whatever soft and fluffy bed you've been laying about in the night before." He stomped over to them. "I don't have to explain myself to you; this is how it's been for the elders of the woodsmen since time immemorial. The young hunt and pay their homage to the old because they're more capable of it." His face was like a mask of iron, forged anger under cooled rage. "We are the last of the Iliarad'ouran elves, the last of our kind to follow our ancient ways—"

"The last of us to follow our outmoded ideas," Martaina tossed out, blistering with sarcasm and feeling her own surprise as she said it, "to sit around campfires at night, sleeping on a hard dirt bed while the rest of the Kingdom sleeps in proper ones."

Amalys's face went from angry to shocked in a heart's beat. "And plays slave to their King as well. Is that what you want? To be one of his sheep, doing his bidding so you can give away half of what you spend your days toiling on?"

"It might be worth the trade," Martaina said rather archly, trying to pull back her surprise at mouthing off. *That's not like me. Not at all.* "Living in a house that's not a lean to, not having to worry about being rained on or living in a cave when the torrential downpours of spring and summer come along, maybe working your way to having servants who could do menial chores for you—"

"You," Amalys said, "aren't of the sort that would ever get a servant of your own. The Kingdom you speak of is a carefully constructed farce; those born low never climb higher. And, my girl, you can't get any lower than being born a woodsman of Iliarad'ouran." His face darkened. "You may think that it'd be nice to live in a manor or on a farm, but they'll never let you have it. Not ever, no chance."

Martaina bit back her bitter desire to spit in his face that she would have it, without doubt. "How would you know?" she asked instead, letting her voice drop to cooler than the running creek on a winter's morn. "You've never ventured beyond the borders of the woods to find out what it's like."

Amalys's eyes flashed with anger. "Go ahead and leave then. Not for a night, or for a week, but for good. Go seek your fortunes, see how it works for you out there." He waved his hand toward the borders of the woods, somewhere beyond their sight. "You'll be back and begging to never leave again within a fortnight."

Martaina said nothing. *I won't rise to his goad. I won't make a rash decision, no matter how much I want to throw it into his face.*

"I thought not," Amalys said after a moment, clearly unimpressed. "Well, go on, then. Get the camp together." He walked a half pace away then turned back. "After all, daylight's burning." He paced off, his walking stick cast aside and forgotten, without a hint of a limp.

"I didn't think you'd actually say that to him," Gareth whispered a moment later.

"Neither did I," Martaina replied, feeling a burning in her throat from all the words she wished she'd been brave enough to say but hadn't. "Neither did I."

Five

The campfire blazed with near-smokeless wood, and Martaina sat next to it, the deer on a spit and roasting as the sun's light began to die. Amalys had disappeared shortly after their argument, not a word more said. The chirp of insects in the air was loud as dusk grew into darkness, and the shadows of the trees went longer and longer with each passing minute. The canopy above them shrouded them from seeing the sky save for just a hint of purple between boughs here and there. Martaina rolled the spit idly with one hand while Gareth sang a simple song almost under his breath.

"Ye old maid of Iliarad'ouran
Walks the woods with mournful heart
She knows well her love betrayed her
And soon enough she'll lay her down.

Gloom of woods, and fog of bleakness
Dusk's last cry shall call her forth
Give her respite from her sadness
A moment's pause in life forlorn."

"Lay off," Martaina said, sending Gareth a thin-lipped look of annoyance. "Unless you want to find this spit up your backside, rolling you over the flames."

Gareth's surprise turned to an instant grin. "Bit touchy, are we? You've never minded my singing before."

"That song is depressing," Martaina replied, looking at the flesh of the animal on the spit, the flames gradually cooking the meat and filling the air with a smell that was making her empty stomach even more ravenous. "Try something with more cheer, like 'The Three Lads of Bleiharth.'"

"Feeling the words coming back upon you like a waterfowl coming south for the winter?" Gareth asked with that same cocksure grin. Martaina kept a tight lid on her irritation.

"I don't notice any parallels, no," Martaina said and took another whiff of the doe. It was nearly ready. "Although I sometimes wonder if you're the maid in question."

"I'm hardly a maid," Gareth said, a little tight-lipped.

"You're hardly anything else," Martaina replied. "Or have you much to report from your last night's sojourn?"

Gareth almost sputtered but caught himself in time, going prim again. "Wouldn't you like to know?"

"I am a mite curious, yes," she said, and took a sniff, trying to catch some hint of any other presence on him. Gareth was a tough one to scent, sometimes bathing up to five times per day to "wash off the grime," as he put it. She eyed his hands; they were scrubbed clean of any of the residual dirt that habitually took up residence under her nails and caked onto her skin. "Does that make me nosey?"

"More than a little." Gareth shifted to lay sideways across the ground. "My business is my own."

"Your liaisons are your own, more like." Martaina twisted the spit once more even as she twisted him. "Unless you're conducting some form of banking in the night."

"However you'd like to say it," Gareth said, and now his grin was gone, replaced by a look of thin amusement. "Would you like to swap tales of ill-refined acts done under the moon's light for sheerest titillation?"

"No," Martaina said, though she felt a hint of a flutter at that thought. "No, I'm merely curious what draws my brother woodsman away in the evenings, whose pull takes him from this way of life we few remaining have embraced to call our own." She felt herself wince. "We lowest of the low."

"There are lower," Gareth said, staring into the fire, "but not much. Not in this King's new order. Field hand peasants are accorded more respect than we of the woods."

"I suppose that's the problem with a society that's so ordered and classed," Martaina said, watching Gareth's regretful stare, "someone has forever got to be on the bottom in everyone's estimation."

"Do you remember the day that Yeram left?" Gareth said with a half-smile, as though remembering something pleasant. "Or were you too young?"

"I remember it vaguely," Martaina said. She remembered Yeram, a kindly woman of almost five thousand years, one who had lived the life of the Iliarad'ouran for all of hers. Martaina recalled the woman's rough hands, turned gentle in an instant to caress her cheeks when she was a child, or her deep, throaty voice singing her a lullaby. "I remember she feared the turn."

"Aye," Gareth said. "We told you as much at the time, but there was more. She said she'd grown weary of being a burden."

"Of being a burden to us?" Martaina asked, the doe forgotten for a moment.

"No," Gareth said, "she meant to the elves, by 'leeching' off this new Kingdom as we do."

"Funny how we call it a 'new' Kingdom when it's been around for longer than both of us," Martaina said with a sly smile.

"Yes, indeed," Gareth said. "Anyhow, she gave a long tract about how Arkaria was changing around us, about how our ways were dying because people no longer wanted to live in the woods, in the wilds—"

"Not that there's much in the way of wilds left around here," Martaina added.

Gareth ignored her and went on. "She said our way of life was going to die, and she didn't want to watch."

"Whatever happened to her?" Martaina asked.

"Not sure," Gareth said. "She went to that upstart new city in the east. Termina, I think they call it."

"Termina," Martaina whispered. She'd heard the name, but it was so far away as to defy even imagining. She could scarcely imagine Pharesia, which she'd seen from time to time, stone walls standing tall and proud, bare earthen fields all around it. She'd heard her father talk about how there had once been woods surrounding the city, how it had been nestled in the heart of the forest before the farmers and loggers had come in and cleared it all out at the King's behest. "How big do you suppose it is, Termina? Is it as big as Pharesia?"

"Surely not," Gareth said with his smirk returned, full force. "It's but a fraction of the size, still being new. It was a fishing village only a dozen years ago, I hear."

"Hm," Martaina said and let it go. She stared at the fire, turning over a thought before looking back to Gareth. "*Are* we going to die out?" She watched him, saw the slight ripple of expression on his face that he quickly buried. "The woodsmen, I mean—"

"I know what you mean." Gareth propped his head up with one hand, his long hair twisted through his fingers. "No, we won't die out." His eyes narrowed and he looked up at her with a simmering bellyful of anger. "The people will realize they've been fooled, one by one. You hear about these changes, about these Dukes and Counts, lording it all over the people, about how unhappy the workers are as they toil the fields, knowing they'll never do anything but work for the men who hold their yolks all their lives. This glorious kingdom that was promised, with Barons to see over each fiefdom, and Lords to look over each county, and masters to watch each house—it is all a lie. They get beds and shelter, grain and barley drink, but they lose themselves." Now Gareth's eyes looked far off, like he was watching something in the distance. "Men and women aren't made to live like that, always at the call of another, not when there's freedom to be had." He took a deep breath. "The filthy air in Pharesia could never compare to this. Some baker's bread could never be traded for a life of berries in the spring, a fresh kill you brought down yourself roasting over a fire." He made a face, mouth downturned. "No master telling you what to do with every hour of your day in exchange for little pieces of metal could ever hold up to the freedom of finishing your hunt for the day and spending the rest of the night by the fire, whiling away the hours with a story and a song."

Martaina thought about it for a moment, heard the conviction in his voice as he said it, and watched the wistful look on Gareth's face as she took to turning the spit again. "True enough," she said at last. "So long as the song isn't 'The Maid of Iliarad'ouran.'"

He gave her a small smile as he looked at her through the fire, his eyes filled with a smoke that didn't come from the conflagration before them.

Six

Martaina took a deep breath of the sweaty night air, the confined space of Nethan's bedchamber far different from staring up at the canopy of the woods, and the faint stars that shone through beyond. The dark ceiling hung overhead, barely visible in the low light of the lamps that streamed in around the cracks in the doors from the hall. Martaina felt Nethan's warmth against her skin, smelled the sweat of the day and kissed him hard on the mouth, taking out her frustrations on his lips.

"Oh, my," Nethan said when she broke off from him, rolling over to the edge of the four-post bed. Their shadow against the light streaming from the frame of the door made her think of trees in the first rays of sunrise. "You have been saving up your energies since last we saw each other." He let out a little breath. "Though I admit, I had not thought a mere two days and one night enough to get you quite so worked up. Still, again you impress me with your boundless energy. So different from a field hand, worn down by the labors of the day."

Martaina felt her back stiffen. "Do you often bed the field hands?"

There was a sort of pause that came before an indifferent reply. "From time to time, it's happened. They certainly lack your vigor." She felt his hand run across her shoulder, a reassuring sort of pat. "The townswomen as well." She felt him lean against her shoulder and kiss her bare skin smoothly. "I've never been with anyone who does what you do."

She tried to force her muscles to relax, but it did not come easily. "Thank you." There was discomfort in her voice, and she traced it to her gut, to the queasy feeling that sprang from his mention of field hands and townswomen in his bed. "Why have you never asked me about my prior lovers?"

"Eh?" Nethan's tone was light surprise. "I've never thought to concern myself with your earlier affairs." He kissed her shoulder again. "I'm only interested in this one." His thin fingers made their way across her face, tilting her chin toward him. He kissed her, waited for her to respond, then broke off gently after a moment.

"Nethan," she said as she heard the wood frame of the bed squeak while he shifted his weight, "what would you say if I told you I might leave the woods?"

"I think you're out of the woods right now." His voice was filled with humor.

"I mean permanently," she said, with greatest reluctance, feeling as though speaking the words aloud was the greatest betrayal. "What if I were to leave the woods permanently?"

"And go where?" his answer came almost immediately.

"I don't know," she said, lying most deliberately, waiting to see what he would say. "Where would a girl like me be welcomed?"

"I can think of a few places," he said, nuzzling his smooth chin against her. So different from her father or Gareth, with their bearded cheeks. "Smaller villages would welcome aid from such a strong lass as you, someone to help manage the game for the local lords. Some guilds of adventurers would surely love assistance from one so skilled in the bow and the trail as you. Why, they've even established a League in Pharesia now for training rangers who do much the same as you, but more for archery in the course of war. They call themselves the Wanderers' Brotherhood." He sniffled in the night air, the stuffy heat of the chamber. "Or you could always go to Termina. I've heard everyone can find a place there."

"Hm," she said, not hearing the option she'd wanted from him. "Termina. Pharesia."

"Well, only that very narrowly defined section of Pharesia," he cautioned. "It's a very hidebound place, very class and status conscious. Newcomers find little favor in polite society unless they come from landed nobility." He hesitated. "I don't think an Iliarad'ouran would find much favor there outside of the Brotherhood."

"I see," she said and rolled over in the bed, clutching the sheet tightly to her breast. She turned her back to him and listened to see if he would say anything else.

He didn't, and the sound of gentle snoring filled her ears only moments later. She lay there, unable to sleep, the softness of the bed deceptively uncomfortable, wishing with all that was in her that she was laying on the forest floor instead.

Seven

"I'm going to go with you on your hunt this morning," Amalys announced a few days later, surprising her as she made ready to leave the camp.

"All right," she said a bit guardedly, watching his face for any sign of a jest, as though he'd simply announce with a laugh that he was fooling her, that he'd really remain in camp as he had for the last eight or more years while she and Gareth did the hunting. She felt a sort of forced discomfort; dealing with her father around the fire at night or during the day was a normal thing and enjoyable in its way when things weren't tense between them. Lately, though, they'd felt tense all the time, and Gareth seemed to be gone even more than she was.

Amalys already had his bow at the ready, an old gnarled thing that looked as though it had been restrung. She peered at him, in his old cloak with his newly prepared bow, and wondered at the change. "I'll lead," he announced and flitted past her with surprising speed, trotting off at a jog.

The smell of the woods was damp and pleasant, a rain the night before having quelled much of the noise. The dry crackle of the leaves was replaced by the occasional drip of a bead of water falling from the canopy above. She could hear a squirrel chattering in the branches somewhere in the distance.

The day was warming, the sun heating the air around her and giving her cause to sweat beneath her cloak. The acidic taste of hunger pushed her on, making her wish she could shove her father aside and follow the sound of the squirrel to his place in the trees, shoot him out of it with one good arrow. She'd surely have to hunt again later, but it'd be a nice enough bite for breakfast to take the edge off the hunger.

Amalys waited for her to come close, looking back over his shoulder at her as he navigated a fallen log to cross a stream. He waited, perched at the end of the tree, the roots all spread out in front of him. He looked at home, she thought, oddly at peace crouched on a tree. He spoke when she came into close range, his voice a whisper low enough to keep from spooking any nearby game. "My legs had forgotten their strength, I've been invaliding by the fire for so long."

"Is that so?" she asked in a low murmur. "I hadn't noticed."

"You need not be false, my daughter," Amalys said, taking to his feet and leaping lightly off the log, making a little noise as he landed, then looked up to her with a cringe on his face. She could tell he knew he'd erred, but he was years out of practice. She gave him a gentle smile, a little forced, and he went on a bit slower. "I have done little to aid you and Gareth in your hunts these last years."

"As is your right as Elder," she said but felt herself repeating his chosen words only, with none of the feeling.

"The Elders of my day were old men, long past the turn," Amalys said, crouching as he stalked along, allowing room for Martaina to follow just in his wake, as they had done in the days when he taught her to hunt. "They were men nearing six millennia, with the creases of age on their faces like the gnarled bark of the oldest trees in the woods." He flashed her a smile. "I am far behind them in age, though I do feel worn like I imagine they did. Though less, I think, from the weariness of a long life and more from the aches and pains of a life spent watching all I love diminished."

"Aye," Martaina agreed, surveying the uneven ground ahead of her. There was a dip where an old stream had flowed perhaps decades ago, now overgrown by weeds. She'd found a few herbs and spices there in the past and a weed that made an excellent salve for blisters.

"I pray to the gods that you not see half the diminishment of our people in your life as I have in mine," Amalys went on, pausing in a thicket of long grass. "It would not take much, of course, since I have seen our people all but wiped out. Only the three of us remain now, but I would find it a terrible tragedy if you and your brood were to see the end of our days."

"I have no brood, father," Martaina said with deep amusement, her fingers running over a blade of long fal'thes grass, taking it between her fingers and stroking it idly.

"But you will," he said without looking at her. "As our people long have, our women finding good seed where they may and taking the children unto their own to be raised here in the woods, steeped in our ways." He glanced back at her with equal measures discomfort and impatience, as though he wanted little to have this conversation.

"Of course," she said awkwardly, not deigning to mention the foul brew that Nethan had introduced her to, ventra'maq, the enchanter's mixture that he had promised would keep his seed from quickening within her. She had never worried about any such thing in her past endeavors with other men; it was expected among the Iliarad'ouran that any child conceived would be raised in their ways, by her, Amalys and Gareth. As it had been since the beginning of their days.

Amalys moved on, stalking low, the faint sound of something ahead of them and upwind. Martaina took a deep sniff, trying to decide if it was a raccoon. It smelled far different, though it was clearly not moving at the moment. She could scent the earthy aroma of fur matted with dirt. She wondered if it was a boar, though those were rare, having been hunted in these grounds to near-extinction several millennia earlier.

The woods were a curious place, bereft of many animals that had once been there, hunted low back when the woodsmen were still strong and Pharesia was growing but had not yet turned to domesticated livestock for its needs. Many of the woodsmen had left the fold during those winnowing days, when all that was left were few deer, small game, and occasionally fish, before the larger streams were cut off to them by the King's guards.

Martaina followed her father, taking care not to disturb so much as a blade of grass as she went, now up on her feet in only a slight crouch. Amalys was bent lower than she, her slightly shorter frame allowing her to keep naturally closer to the ground. She had gotten her height from her father, she'd always heard, though she'd never met her mother to be certain.

Amalys suddenly stopped, holding an arm out stiff for her to do the same as she sniffed the air again, unable to see past him to find out what had gotten him to halt in such a hurry. It was an unfamiliar scent, something she had not encountered before. She tried to see around him but he turned to her, now squatting down to hide his outline, and she hesitated only a moment before following so she could glimpse for herself what awaited them.

It was a bear.

Martaina thought she could recall seeing one in her youth, a triumph for the Iliarad'ouran in the waning days when there were still a handful of them remaining, before Yeram left, back when the twins were still hunting with them, before those two had left to go north for some reason she'd not understood as a child. She remembered the bear carcass being dragged into camp when she was still too young to be on the hunt herself, back when she chafed at having to wait at camp, to prepare the food that the hunters brought back while they reveled in the day's successes. She caught herself drawing a deep breath and held it, eyeing the black-furred animal pawing at a stump.

Her father had already unslung his bow and had it nocked, and Martaina did the same, mirroring him. They looked sidelong at each other as Martaina slid into place next to him. For an animal this large both of them would fire and fire again, working in coordination to bring it down before it could run away. She saw the gleam of excitement in his eyes and knew she had a similar one in her own. The last bear had sent a thrill through the camp that had lasted for weeks, had reinvigorated the last of them like nothing else before or since.

She drew back her bow and looked down the shaft of the arrow at her target. It would be an easy shot, the bear only twenty or so paces away. She thought about waiting for her father to fire first but ultimately released in a hurry.

The arrow slung through the air, followed less than a second later by Amalys's. They whipped through the intervening space, the bear roaring with fury as her arrow impacted between his ribs and her father's landed in the thick meat of his back. She fired again after only the briefest pause, enough time to grasp an arrow by the fletching and nock it, drawing the string back and checking her aim before letting it fly.

This one impacted in the side of the bear's neck, the broadhead causing the beast to jerk and grunt in pain as a spurt of blood geysered out from beneath the black fur. Her father's second shot was aimed almost the same as his first and buried itself in the meat of the animal's back.

The bear grunted and began a long, loping run on all four legs that was, she imagined, more ponderous and labored than it would have been before the arrows hit. It slowed as it went, and she planted another arrow in its hindquarters, her father doing the same. It slowed to a desperate pace, dragging the last bit of distance before it fell.

Martaina exchanged a look of satisfaction with Amalys, his eyes gleaming and a broad smile under his dark beard splitting his face. "I suppose I should come hunting more often, eh?"

Martaina paused before answering. "We do seem to have had good luck with your presence. I haven't ever even seen a sign of one of these creatures, let alone run across one of them."

"We're deeper in the woods now than we've been in some time," Amalys said as they stood and slowly worked their way toward the bear.

They approached hesitantly; it was likely still alive, and moving at it too quickly might allow it to land a fearsome strike on one of them. Giving it time to bleed out while death settled upon it was far more preferable, keeping the animal from running off again. "Doubtful we would have ever seen it had we not been forced to move camp."

"Aye," Martaina agreed.

"Can you imagine what Gareth will say when he returns?" Amalys's voice was quivering with excitement of a kind she could not recall hearing since she was a child. "Do you even remember when last we brought a bear back to camp?" He did not wait to see her nod assent. "It put a fire and food in our bellies that lasted for quite some time." He was bursting with pride. "Months, even. I still sleep under the skin on the coldest nights." She nodded, well aware of the bear and the story behind it. He grinned at her. "This one can be yours. Your own."

She felt a little numbness at the thought. Only a year earlier she would have been smiling with a wide grin of her own, but now her enthusiasm was muted, as though it were a fire that had had a bucket of water dumped upon it. "Yes," she said finally, but Amalys did not even notice.

"Come on, then," Amalys said, outpacing her now toward the fallen form. "We'll dress it out here and get a sling ready. It'll take both of us to haul it back." He reached the side of the creature, moving quietly, then gingerly slit its throat when he arrived at the side of it. He did it quickly, and the bear stirred only a little, the last of its vigor nearly gone now.

She stood back while Amalys did the dressing, removing the guts and emptying out its belly. "Time was we could have found uses for all this," he said. "But not now, not with so few of us and so many things easily available by barter." He turned his face toward his task at hand, cleaning it out quickly as Martaina pulled rope from her pack, tying the legs and readying it for dragging.

They said little as they dragged it back to camp, her father glowing with the pride of the first kill he'd been on in years, Martaina still too stunned to believe what they'd done. *A bear. A real, live bear, like something out of the old stories.*

It took them almost two hours to get back to camp, and Amalys's enthusiasm did not diminish one whit on their way. "This is just what we needed," he said as the camp drew into sight. "The forest has provided for the Iliarad'ouran once more."

Martaina nodded her agreement, feeling the burn of the rope even through the gloves she wore for dragging the sling. The bear was heavy and her muscles were already weary from yesterday's long trek back to the camp from Nethan's plantation. She had thought herself in fine condition for such things, but the longer distances had begun to wear on her, her hip moaning protestations in a place where she'd hurt it against a tree while running a few months prior.

"Gareth!" Amalys shouted as they dragged the big animal right into the heart of the encampment. "Gareth, turn out! You won't believe what we've got!" He let a cackle of warm enthusiasm, an infectious sound that made Martaina smile even in spite of her aches. She dropped the ropes as they settled the bear into place next to the fire, and gave herself a moment to stretch before she looked about, wondering if Gareth had made it back from his prior night's activities.

"Confound that boy," Amalys said under his breath. "Caught the smell of sweet honey in some city tart's hair, the yeast of some baker's daughter, and it pulls him out of the woods." He clapped his rough hands together. "He'll be in for a surprise when he returns."

Martaina felt a rough drop of her stomach, the sudden, unfortunate gasp of her insides as she caught sight of a scrap of parchment laid out on the ground where Gareth's bedroll had been when they left. She took a step closer to it, a lone piece of flat parchment torn from something, with writing on one side in rough letters, all Gareth's unstudied hand was probably capable of producing. Martaina knew the letters, had learned to read from the only book her father owned, from hours of instruction by Yeram. She shook her head and clapped Amalys on the shoulder once to get his attention.

Amalys looked from her to the scrap on the ground, looking down at it and cocking his head. "What's this?" He asked, staring at it, dumbstruck.

Martaina let out a breath she didn't realize she'd been holding and stared at it for a moment before looking away and turning her gaze to the horizon, scanning the forest for any sign of life. She wondered if Gareth was still out there, watching to see if they'd gotten it, then dismissed that thought. *He wouldn't have waited around, not if his mind was made up.* She looked back down to it and read it again, a single word by itself, followed by Gareth's own scrawled name.

Farewell.

Eight

One Thousand Years Later

Martaina caught the scent again, edging closer to a defined trail. The edge of the Waking Woods was creeping ever nearer, and she cursed mildly, under her breath. *I do not want to go in there. Not tonight.* She sighed and looked back at the hunting party following her. It had been months of action in Luukessia followed by days of defense across the Endless Bridge, a terror chasing her every waking moment and every sleepless night.

The Scourge.

She could see their grey faces when she closed her eyes, the horror of them still fresh in her mind as she'd fired every arrow she had at them and been left with nothing when they'd returned to Sanctuary. They were an implacable foe, the sure destruction of everything she'd ever known and come to care about.

Meanwhile, the dark elves were here, trying to destroy everything I care about. She felt the glowing embers of her rage inside, a slow burn of fury that kept her driving on even though she desired nothing more than to retire to her chambers and sleep, possibly for a decade, to return to a state of non-fatigue. She wished for a millberry plant, the leaves of which could be crumpled and placed under the tongue to increase one's alertness. It was something she had learned from the Wanderers' Brotherhood after a lifetime of passing it by as a tasteless weed.

"He's gone into the woods, hasn't he?" Longwell's voice was tentative but hopeful. She looked back to see him close at hand, Thad back a ways now, talking with three of the warriors from Sanctuary who had accompanied the hunting party.

"He has," Martaina said, trying to keep herself indifferent to the King of Galbadien's words. She looked back at the faintest hint of a trail, the trampled grass and spots of blood that were leading to the forest's edge. "He's not terribly far ahead now, though. We'll catch him in the next half hour if we hurry on."

"Very well," Longwell said with excessive stiffness. He was always a stern fellow, his every expression a guarded one, save for a very few, very occasional few. He leaned in closer to her, to speak. "About—"

"We are in the midst of a hunt for a dark elven officer," she said, as though she needed to remind him.

He almost flinched, blinking back his surprise at her words, which she suspected had come close to a rebuke. His face showed a hint of expression, hardly the most she had seen from him in the last months, but surely more than anyone else had. "I will tend to my duty, you need not fear for that."

"Good," she said and turned away from him. "All else need wait for a different occasion."

"Very well," Longwell said, and she heard the hint of disappointment in his voice. His soft footfalls carried him back to his horse, and she listened to them, every one. It was unusual for a man of the sword to walk so softly, in her experience.

But then again, until him, never had she had a man so noble and high who hadn't turned away from her in shame at the first morning's light, either. A King, no less, though of a land now dead and lost.

Martaina ducked her head low and put it down, sighing out her frustration, her fatigue, and taking another deep inhalation of the night air. The chill mixed with her tiredness, and all she wanted was to get beneath a blanket and find a wagon to take her back to Sanctuary, wrapped up in the warmth until she could lie before the hearth in her chamber and sleep, just sleep in her soft bed.

Instead she forced that image out of her head and breathed in again. She smelled the blood and put one unsteady foot in front of another as she went back to the trail, careful to mind her walk so her feet didn't betray her. Careful to keep herself steady, she paced after him, this dark elf, this enemy that she would hunt down just as surely as if he were any other beast that she'd been called on to slay.

Nine

One Thousand Years Earlier

Amalys had been quiet, mutterings only occasionally escaping as they'd skinned the bear. He'd said nothing for the first hour, nothing at all, had just worked as they'd cut up the meat, readied some of it to be dried, and cut up other parts for immediate frying. Martaina had saved some fat from the beast that she'd culled out as they'd worked it, and the fire was already going. She was prepared to make a gravy from it, something to add some flavor to the meat.

"He'll be back," Amalys said with a certainty that Martaina thought bordered on delusion. "He's lived his whole life among us." There was no hint of the desperation she felt certain she'd have let slip under the circumstances, and though it should have worried her, it didn't. "He doesn't know any other way." Amalys licked his lips, and Martaina watched him, wondering if it was simple nerves or something else. "He'll see soon enough that the greenest fields always belong to someone else. When you have to tend to them yourself, they suddenly lose their verdancy."

"I don't think he much cares about that," Martaina said quietly then halted, scarcely believing she'd said it.

Amalys didn't respond at first, favoring her with a near-suspicious look. "Oh? How's that?"

Well, now I've said it. Might as well finish it. "He was lonely, father. The kind of all-consuming lonely that drives a man to find a companion."

"Nonsense," Amalys said, shaking his head stubbornly. "He could have had his little side dishes and still come back to us. Like you have. Like I did, in my day." His beard swung as he shook his head. "That's how we grow after all. That's how I ended up with you. You go out and have your fun and bring the child back to the woods for proper raising—"

"Not everyone wants to give up their child to the Iliarad'ouran, Father," Martaina said, not meeting his eyes.

"You think you're being coy with me," Amalys said with a low irritation. "Let's be truthful, daughter of mine. In the Kingdom of the Elves, no one wants to admit to having a child born of one of us. We are the lowest rung of the ladder. Far from the days when we were the most exalted and children were given up to us to be trained with skill and honor as woodsmen and women, now they're given up by our partners because we're outcasts and would taint their precious world with the stink of our labors and the blood of our prey."

Martaina said nothing. "They're not all like that. They don't all see us that way."

"They're all like that now," Amalys said, cutting forcefully into a piece of meat as he shaved some of the excess fat off it. "When I was young, they weren't. Now it's different. You know it's different." He looked up at her and she felt a charge with his words. "Any man who beds you in this age is merely lowering himself for the satisfaction of his loins."

She threw down her knife and tossed aside the lump of fat she'd been working loose, throwing it into the cauldron with a soft plopping noise. She stood and felt the fury settle in her heart, in her stomach. "I am not some harlot meant only to pleasure a man and nothing else. You know nothing, old man. The world has run fast around you while you breathe the smoke of your fires out here in the woods and take poppy milk to heal your imaginary aches. There are people out there who don't consider themselves lower than anyone else, who do kindnesses to others and for others, who would offer even us—your perceived lowest—a place in the Kingdom of the Elves where we need not forage the greens and hunt the woods every night for sustenance. This land is not as you see it in your shallow view, and there is more out there waiting than ever could be found within these borders."

"So you think, mine daughter?" Amalys said, but there was a weariness about him. "I wish it were so. I think even withdrawn as I am, I know more about this world of yours and its people than you do." He looked east, back toward Pharesia, back toward their old camp, and she heard him sigh. "More of them are like those guards we met than like this shining vision of which you speak." He waved a hand at her, reserving his knife in the other hand as though jealously guarding it. She suspected he was trying to be as non-threatening as possible. "But if you truly believe that, why not go seek your interest elsewhere? Why not go find your own greener fields?"

She stood stiffly, feeling like she was seeing him for the first time. He looked weak, a hint uncertain. "Perhaps I will do that very thing," she said, and took her skinning knife and sheathed it without even wiping it clean first.

"Go on, then," he said, his voice sounding a bit high and thin. "Go ask this man what he would have you do if you were to leave the woods. Ask him if he would be your husband, make a wife of you. See what he says. See if I'm wrong." Amalys began to look smaller as she started to walk away, casting a look back to watch him as he kept talking. "Ask him, and I'll see you again on the morrow when you find out the truth of things out there."

"No, you won't," she breathed and quickened her pace. She could still smell the hint of the bear's scent on her, but where only hours ago she would have thought it so rare, so fanciful as to be barely believed and celebrated, now she could scarcely stand the smell of it on her dirty hands.

Ten

"I had not thought I would see you tonight," Nethan said after they'd finished, still sighing into the darkness. "Not that I'm complaining." He shifted in the bed, disturbing her with his motion. "Though it was a bit of a long day in the fields."

"Oh?" she asked, trying to find a way to circle around to what she wanted to ask him that wouldn't seem callous or too forward. *Would you marry me?*

"I'm afraid so," Nethan intoned, not catching her intention. "We had to let go a few field hands today due to poor performance. They're a bit farther up there in the years, close to the turn, and they slow down considerably after a certain point."

"Could I ever be your wife?" Martaina asked, the words spilling out like the blood from the bear's neck after the arrow pierced it.

"I ... *what?*" Nethan's face visibly paled, even in the darkness.

"Would you," Martaina said, not daring to look at him, instead keeping her eyes fixed on the ceiling above, with its odd white sculpting, "ever make an Iliarad'ouran your wife?"

"Uhm," Nethan said, almost stuttering, "you are ... certainly a balm to me. Great comfort—"

"So I'm fit to be a comfort woman," Martaina said, not letting any emotion spill out, "but not a wife."

Nethan seemed taken aback. "I ... I ... never thought we'd even need to discuss this, but ... I mean ... I'm a planter. I would have to marry a woman of my station or higher else I'd lose my place in society—"

"I see," Martaina said, and the heat in her body was intense, more than any time she could recall. The torrent of emotions was almost more than she could bear, lying there with the sheets tangled about her, the curious sense of shame and desire pooling in her. She repressed the urge to twitch with anxiety, to vibrate her leg with nervous energy.

"I am sorry," Nethan said, and she could see he had turned to her now, in her peripheral vision. "I didn't know that you'd ever even considered it a possibility—"

"It's fine," she said and rolled toward him. She looked him over once, his fine, bronzed skin still as appealing to her as it had been before, his handsome face sown with regret, an expression of deepest sorrow turning his lips down in a pained look. "It's all right," she said again and kissed him with a fiery passion that was hotter than any of the times she'd kissed him before. He resisted at first, his eyes still open when she looked, but a few moments of caresses and he gave in.

She steered the course the whole time, never once letting him have a moment of control. She taxed him long, listened to him moan for a release that she never gave him. Once she was done she simply stopped and stared down at him. There was a moment's hesitation in his eyes, as though he expected her to go on. She looked at him, thinking about him as she would a animal she stalked, and rolled off, not even breathing heavily.

"Why did you stop?" he asked as her feet touched the ground. She fumbled for her animal skins and threw them on, one by one.

"Because I'm done," she replied as she stood and pulled up her breeches, snugging the rope belt tight.

"Oh," he said, uncertain, his face crumpled. She wondered if he'd say anything further in protest. He did not. She laced up the front of her shirt, watching him the entire time. He didn't meet her gaze, didn't say anything, still looking like he'd been shamed.

She fastened her cloak around her neck, hoisted the quiver up along with the bow, and then looked back. Her hand went to her knife and she realized as her fingers caressed the hilt that it was still dirty, still covered in animal fat and meat, and she crossed back over to the bed in three long strides and kissed Nethan once more.

When she broke he looked up at her with true bewilderment. "What was that for?"

"To remember you by," she said and then drew the knife and placed it across his neck.

"Please don't," he hissed in utter fear. She could smell the night scents, the air was thick with the aroma of their lovemaking, though it hadn't been love, she knew. "I am so sorry."

"You will never tell anyone what I've done with you," Martaina said, low and long, and watched a little drop of blood well up at the end of the blade where she had it pressed into his throat. "I am ashamed of myself for the nights I've spent lowering myself to be with you. If anyone ever asks, you've never heard my name, never known my touch, and never had me grace your bed." She applied a gentle pressure. "Should so much as a rumor ever reach my ears about an Iliarad'ouran woman and a planter, you shall never see the arrow that brings you low, but you'll feel every cut of my knife as I drag you into the woods and flay you alive." She sniffed deep, remembered the scent of the moment, the fear, his eyes wide. "You may not be able to countenance the thought of me as your wife, but I cannot tolerate the thought of anyone ever believing we were lovers."

With that she sheathed her blade in one smooth motion, the pungent scent of the meat that she'd cut with it lost beneath the smell of all that had happened in the room, in the bed.

"I'm sorry, Martai—"

"Never say my name again," she said, stepping into the shadow in front of the door. Light streamed from the frame around her, but she knew that he'd be blinded by it, that she'd be cloaked in the shadow it made of her. "Never so much as whisper it aloud."

"I'm sorry, nonetheless," Nethan whispered. "If it were a different time or place—"

"It is not," she said with utter softness, the harshness heavy even on her ears. "Do not ever pretend it to be otherwise, not to any other woman, lest you find someone with less restraint than I." With that, she hurled open the door and left, without so much as the squeak of a floorboard to herald her flight from the plantation house.

Eleven

She crossed the darkened woods without worrying about being quiet. Birds flew before the sound of her steps, something she never would have allowed in the day. The chirp of insects echoed in her ears along with Nethan's words. She felt a heat on her cheeks even these long miles later that contrasted with the night air. The miles passed as the same thoughts repeated themselves over and over without pause, like a ceaseless cawing of crows at daybreak while one was trying to sleep.

She passed through a brook without caring that her feet became chill, she brushed through a patch of fal'thes grass and felt loose blades stick to the wet hides she walked in. At one point she felt nauseous, as though she might loose her empty stomach, but it never happened.

She knew the woods well, the distances involved, and even in her distraction she knew when she was close. A faint glow in the distance heralded the campfire, and the sickly feeling she carried within softened slightly at the knowledge that she was home now, and she would not have to leave the woods again should she not desire to.

A moan that cut through the night air, through the sound of insects, caused her to brush back her long hair, exposing her pointed ears. She cocked her head and listened, and heard the same sound again, that same faint moan in the distance, from the campfire. She thought it curious at first then heard a companion voice come along with it. She slowed her pace, edging closer to the fire, but not so close yet she could see if anyone was around it. The voices carried much farther than her sight, yet she could not discern with her eyes what she was looking at, not in the dark, not with the shadows cast by the flame's illumination.

She crept closer, believing at first that perhaps Gareth had returned, and felt her heart lighten for but a moment before a crass voice rang out, dispelling that illusion. It was not the sound of Gareth's voice, nor Amalys's either. She lowered herself into the grass, going along at a stalking pace, silent movement through the dry leaves and occasional grass.

"A bearskin!" came one of the voices, the loudest one. The crass one. "Where would this crippled old beggar find a bear?"

"Perhaps one of the others hunted it for him," came a suggestion from another voice, as still another laughed in the background. "Where are the others?"

"The other man was seen by the gate guards in Pharesia entering the city at sundown," the crass voice spoke again, disinterested in his own reply and clearly focused on something else. "I had them send word by messenger. And the daughter is with her planter for the night, according to a field hand who I paid some bronze to." A grin crept into the words. "We can go find her next, pay her a visit that she'll remember—"

Martaina nocked and let fly an arrow before the words finished leaving Hesshan's lips, and she was close enough now to see the broadhead penetrate his throat, could hear the odd, wet clicking noise as he tried to keep speaking, lips unaware of what had happened only inches lower. She fired again at one of the others, the arrow catching him in the ear and continuing on through his head to jut out the other side. She fired as quickly as she pulled, a calm precision taking over her as though she were merely dispatching prey in the same manner she had done every day for the last several years of her life. She hit the third with an arrow through the eye, and the last she lungshot as he was running away.

Her breathing was surprisingly calm as she entered the camp. Hesshan's was gasping, his dark skin already slick with blood, pitched over on his back where he'd been sitting, next to Amalys's body. Martaina spared only a look for her father before she gazed upon Hesshan, his guard's tunic of navy blue now looking much darker thanks to the spreading stain down its front. He lay next to the fire, and she gave him a sharp kick, rolling him onto the edge of it. He gasped, the bear skin still clutched in his hands. She watched it catch fire, slowly at first then aided by the flames, it ignited Hesshan's tunic by the sleeves. He gestured wildly, his hands and arms aflame, but she ignored him, stooping to see Amalys.

Her father's face was already pale and cold to her touch. His eyes were open, his tunic of animal skins wet with blood and pierced in four places. He had no weapon in his hand, nor any nearby, and she knew they had caught him unawares, sleeping, or awake and unready to fight back. She stared into his glassy, unseeing eyes, and wondered if she would have even been able to help if she'd been here, or if it simply would have been a slaughter for two instead.

She stepped over him and took his bow, carefully placing it into his hands and across his chest. "Like an Iliarad'ouran," she said, not really sure who she was speaking to. She placed the quiver by his side, then turned back to see Hesshan make his last movement, his body burning with the spread of the fire across his clothing.

Martaina took a last look, surveying, unsentimental, and grabbed the light pack she'd left behind that held a patera and a few spices. She always kept it bound together to make it harder for an animal to get into, but that also made it always ready for travel. She took a sniff and reflected that the smell of Hesshan burning was not so different from an animal roasting on a spit, then calmly walked away. The last of the guardsmen was still alive, writhing and lungshot, so she opened his throat with her dagger as she passed, the cold night air chilling her as she did it.

When she was done she cleaned and sheathed her blade, determining her way from the stars. *East,* she thought and headed back the way she had come.

In the light of the morning sun she caught sight of it, Pharesia, gleaming walls all vine-covered and glorious, the sum of everything she had ever wanted, Nethan and comfortable beds and a life of high finery all in one. She walked toward it until just after sun up, and then turned when she hit the road.

She left the gleaming city behind her as she headed north, losing sight of it by midday, her walk steady and unhurried as she passed under the shaded trees of the Iliarad'ouran's north woods, her face untouched by any emotion at all as she followed the road and its signs toward a place called Termina.

Twelve

One Thousand Years Later

The hunt was drawing to a close, the Waking Woods giving her every sign that her quarry was near. She could hear something thrashing in the underbrush, the shuffling steps of a desperate man kicking up leaves as he stumbled along. The scent of blood was heavier now, the man's wound getting worse with his flight. *He knows we're behind him. He knows his steps are dogged, his minutes are numbered.* She slitted her eyes to squint ahead, the dark of the night total save for the light of the torches carried by the men behind her.

Her hand was on her bow, an arrow at the ready but the string undrawn, simply waiting for the sight of her foe before she used it. Her steps were light and quick in spite of her intense fatigue, drawing her forward toward the end of this business.

She entered a thicket and heard the rustle of her enemy ahead. She caught a glimpse of his shadow and loosed an arrow. She blinked her tired eyes and saw it reach home, the gasp of pain torn from her foe's lips as he was lifted from his feet and thrown to the ground by the force of the arrow. He made a noise, a winded sound that told her he was lung-shot, gasping, and she approached with caution, knife in hand, ready to end the hunt.

He had already rolled to his back, the head of the arrow and the shaft sticking out of his chest. He made a wheezing sound as she approached, the noise of a man not long for the world, and his face carried a dull, flat look, his white hair almost aglow in the light of the torches that followed in her wake.

The dark elf said nothing as she stepped close to him, her knife obvious as his eyes fell to it. He looked from it to her, in obvious pain, his tunic soaked through and bloody. She hesitated just a beat upon seeing him there, laid out, slumped on a root, his upper body at an angle, slightly propped up.

"General Ardin Vardeir," Thad said from behind her, and she could hear his pleasure in the words. "Run to ground like a common dog as he was retreating." There was satisfaction dripping from every word. "We could hang him for what he's done to us these last months, get a measure of pain in return for that he's paid on us—"

Martaina stooped low, keeping her eyes on the General's. His hands were grasping his legs, and he was looking at her dully as she dropped to a knee to get close to him. She looked at him, and the light of the torches her party carried gave his face an orange glow, like he was lit by a campfire. All talk of a hanging was sheer lunacy, she knew; the man was breathing his last breaths.

One of his hands came up from his leg, slowly, and tugged at her sleeve. She looked down at it in slight surprise but did nothing to stop it. He smeared his blood on her tunic; her worn, dirty, ragged tunic that had seen battles too numerous to count since last she had washed it. The cloth was still soft against her skin, nothing like the animal skins she had worn when she learned to hunt. Her legs felt the bite of the hard ground, the root that the General was lying on poking into her knee.

He opened his mouth to say something but failed, only a rasp emerging. The pain around his eyes grew, a faint frustration that was hampered by the agony he was sure to be in. There was a sense of fading light in his eyes, and she saw it, knew the end was close.

"Go on," she said, not breaking eye contact.

He stared at her, his face a mask of pain, then spoke, a soft, wheezing rasp. "Tell ... my daughter ..." His last breath came, a sound that rattled just a little as it left his body. His face went slack, head tilting as his neck lost the fight against his sagging muscles. With surprising gentleness, Martaina eased him to the ground, dragging him off the root so his body could lie prostrate. With a last touch, she closed his eyes.

"So much for that hanging," Longwell said, but he didn't seem too fussed about it.

"It's a shame," Thad said, and the hardness of his words were difficult for Martaina to hear. "What he did to us, to Sanctuary—"

"Is over now," Martaina said as she stood, looking down at the unmoving dark elf.

"I suppose," Thad said, as though he didn't really believe it. "But the dead, the destruction ... the dark elves have truly wrecked our home—"

"Home," Martaina said, rolling the word around in her mouth, ignoring the rest of what Thad said. "I want to go home."

There was a pause, and Longwell was next to speak. "I suppose we can. Should we bring the body back to—?"

"No," Martaina said, and looked down at the corpse once more. "There are plenty enough of them crowding the grounds of Sanctuary as it is. Best leave this one where it lies."

"Wizard," Thad called out, and somewhere in the hunting party Martaina could hear murmured assent from the person Thad called to, "cast us home."

A faint light glowed as the spell began. Martaina looked her last upon the body. The general's eyes were unmoving, no life in them, no steady breathing, his days at an end. He looked ... peaceful, as though he had simply fallen asleep. The light of the torches played across his navy skin, the firelight giving it a hue of liveliness that would surely not last past their leaving. "Goodbye," she whispered, so low that none of the others could hear it, and felt the warmth of the magic as it spread across her skin, carrying her home, and back to a comfortable bed.

A PRINCESS OF SOVAR

You do not know Sovar. Humans hear the name Saekaj Sovar and think of one large city, the dark capital of the shadowed elves, and know naught else of it but a name, a tremble, a fear to wake to in the midst of a nightmare.

Whispers of slavery, of men and women in chains harnessed to some dark purpose, are bandied about in cities of free men like Reikonos, where even the despised dark elves are only occasionally harmed. Reikonos is a pleasure palace for dark elves compared to the horror that would await a human in Saekaj and Sovar, the twin chambers where most of the dark elven population dwell in the darkness beneath the rocky surface of Arkaria. But humans do not know them as separate entities or that they are beneath the soils, that they are in a darkness so complete that any human brought down to the depths goes blind within a matter of mere weeks, stumbling sightlessly for the rest of his days.

No, you do not know Sovar, nor Saekaj either. But I know them. I know them all too well—the wealth and splendor and exclusivity of Saekaj, and the bitter, clutching, ravening poverty of Sovar. I have tasted the latter, tasted it like bitter clay that is all the poorest have to eat on the worst days, and it sits on my tongue like the sediment that it is.

I know Sovar, I knew it well until the day I left—left and never looked back. I know it still because Sovar never changes. It is a fixed point, an unmoving star in the night sky, and remains constant as rain on a summer's day falling across the grasses of Perdamun. I can tell you about Sovar, give you a glimpse into the darkness, let your human eyes see as most never do.

Come with me into the dark, into Sovar, and be illuminated in a way that I never was until the day I escaped from her shadows.

*

I was born in poverty, I lived in poverty, and if I had stayed, fulfilling the wish of the Sovereign for all dark elves to remain in their born stations, I would have died as impoverished as I had begun.

In Reikonos, a dark elf can become a dockworker, save money, become a merchant, perhaps work his way up to owning a farm outside the city. I know of a few dark elves who have even bought houses on the bluffs overlooking the Torrid Sea, a privilege that is supposedly only for humans and the occasional wealthy elf. This happens in blatant defiance of the Council of Twelve's sumptuary laws on the matter, but even they turn a blind eye. Gold is the god of Reikonos, no matter what Virixia or Ashea might receive in the way of temples, and even the Council of Twelve is subject to that particular divinity's good graces.

In Sovar, though, it is said that the rungs on the ladder of opportunity have all been cut out. Certainly, you hear a few tales now and again of those who faithfully serve the Sovereign moving up in the world. Everyone knows the legend of Amenon Lepos, who was born in Sovar, who lived in Sovar, and who rose to take the second-greatest manor in Saekaj. His name is on the lips of every boy in Sovar; all of them want to be him, and all the girls want to marry the next Amenon Lepos before he leaves the squalor behind.

None of them will, though.

The last census taken of the Sovereignty found almost two million people living in the capital, and all but two hundred thousand of them were in Sovar. One hundred and fifty thousand of them are servants who live and work in the manor houses of elite of Saekaj. If not for this then they, too, would be in the depths with the rest of us.

Only one noble—ONE of them—has risen from Sovar.

One in two million.

The rungs of the ladder are indeed removed, misplaced, chopped out so that Saekaj can remain the exclusive club that it has always been. The story of Amenon Lepos keeps the youth hoping, though, until they become too old and beaten down by the workaday labor offered hauling clay or toiling in the pits or fishing the Great Sea below to realize that *they have been deceived*. Even the army officers buy into it in order to live near the Front Gate, the more upper-crust section of Sovar, rather than in the Back Deep. The brightly dyed fabric has been well and truly pulled over their eyes, though; they don't even realize it until they're too worn down to do anything about it.

The people should see the truth of it on the day when the League heads come down from Saekaj to examine all the poor children of Sovar for magical abilities. It's a show, all of it. Once per year they turn us all out from our ramshackle abodes, from our dirt homes cut into the mud or built atop other shanties in the depths of Sovar. They set the time, ring bells in the streets and we all come running—the youth, those not yet broken down by a life of labor—fresh with the possibility of being the next Amenon Lepos.

Fools, all of them, for only a handful are chosen in a good year, and in some years, none at all. There are never any chosen from the Back Deep, that pit of despair on the downward slope of the cavern where the poorest of the poor make their homes. For them, the dream should be dead right then and there.

But it doesn't die, it morphs into the glorious idea of becoming a spearman in the army and somehow worming one's way into the middle class, a small cottage in the Middle Grounds of Sovar, or in the Carved Caves out of the main chamber. Or even a small shell house near the gates of Saekaj, at the lowest end of the elite class. Only one in a generation does this, but it keeps hope alive.

And hope is all we poor fools have.

*

On the day they turned us out in my twelfth year, I was to be subject to the testing. I had woken early, the earliest riser in my shanty, a cloth structure spun from silk webbing on top of a three-story clay home. Eighteen families lived on the four floors, counting the three who shared the tent space on the roof with us. I knew them all now, but they had been strangers when I was assigned the dwelling a few years ago by the Sovar Housing Authority, a fancy name for a man with bad breath who chortled a lot and was flanked by eight guards everywhere he went. I'd heard the women around me curse his name after making certain he wasn't in earshot, and even at the age of twelve I knew he demanded things for choicest housing. He had his favorites, that was certain, and he gave his favors in exchange for things I didn't want to know about. "Foul men beget foul deeds," was an adage I heard early on in life.

I woke in the wee hours of the morning. Through a seam of the tent I could see the phosphorescent glow of the cave ceiling a hundred feet above me. I could hear whispers in the next building, out one of the mud-brick windows, their house not afflicted with a cloth tent on top. A woman on the third floor was one of the favored of the Housing Overseer. Only eight families lived there, on four floors, and the third only had one within its walls. I wondered at the luxury, thinking it couldn't possibly be any better in Saekaj. After all, who could conceive of one family living in one house?

When I woke on the day of the testing, I stared up at the top of the tent for a time. I could hear the snoring of Theratas Gruhm, the kindly old man who lived in the corner of our room with his wife. They were elderly, unable to work as full-time laborers any longer and as a consequence were reduced to petty odd jobs. A lifetime of effort had left Gruhm's hands gnarled and his back bent. His wife did not speak but was much the same, save for the bent back. She had been a seamstress, I was told, and her arthritic knuckles showed it, forever locked into an unmoving position.

Theratas was one of the few who had time for me. I was an orphan, and few even in my own dwelling had any interest in associating with one of the Sovereign's wards, the lowest of the low. Gruhm answered questions, was quick with a smile, and was the only person close to being a friend I had in my home.

After a time of listening to the others in the room breathe, I got up and dressed. I had two dresses, and in this I was fortunate; most of my peers had only one. They were both dyed dramatic colors, as dye was the only thing we had plentiful amounts of in Sovar. It was a byproduct of wildroots, one of the most common and cheapest foods eaten in Sovar, and so it was always available and the color provided a little light in our dreary lives.

I took a deep breath of the stale air, the smell of all the bodies crammed together with only a few chamber pots, not enough to overwhelm me. In the mornings our waste was given to a man who had a special cart to collect it, where it was taken into the pits of the Depths to cultivate mushrooms and beans for our daily ration, which was desperately small. Waste not, still want.

I stuck my face out between the cloth walls of our dwelling, taking care not to step on a child who was sleeping in the corner. My eyes found the city skyline. The shanties gave way in the distance toward the Front Gate—the small, more elite section of Sovar where the mid-ranking officials lived.

They were guard captains, bureaucrats, servants of Saekaj, but they were not allowed to live in the upper chamber. Their mud hut houses were so far up the slope of the cave floor as to be miles away, close to the entrance to the tunnelways that led up to Saekaj and, eventually, the surface. I had never been to either, of course, and wondered what they might be like.

The vast majority of spell casters were in the upper class; of course, the League academies were all in Saekaj. Taking a breath, I dared hope that this day I might indeed see them for myself.

I scraped the last of a sprout and bean stew, the staple diet of Sovar, out of the pot in the corner. It was cold and greasy and slick, and I didn't care. In an hour everyone else would wish that they'd arisen early to get it, and I wouldn't care then, either. The thick aroma of it wafted as I shoved it in my mouth with my fingers, the slick, oily residue running down my chin. When I was done, I used the fractional amount of water I had left to rinse my face. That was a luxury that didn't happen every day, washing one's face (let alone the rest of the body, an unbelievable custom that I found out about in Reikonos later in life). When done, I made my way quietly down the stairs into the house.

I paused at the stairwell on the third floor that led down to the second. Merin Nemy lived below, a spoiled brat of a little girl who had five dresses and never let me forget that I only had two. Her father was a lieutenant in the guards; she never let anyone forget this, either. She was, of course, exactly my age, and involved herself in every single thing that I did. I assumed that this was all so that she could torment me, but I wasn't above heaving a little well-aimed cruelty back at her. She had a very flat nose, an unfortunate feature that made her look a little like a vek'tag—those enormous, lumbering spiders that pulled carts all around Saekaj and Sovar.

And I never let her forget that, either.

I took a breath before I began my descent. If fortune and Yartraak favored me, I'd pass her floor and be on the ground in moments, unhindered by her wicked tongue. If that happened, though, it would be more grace from Yartraak than he'd ever given before. I steeled myself and began to descend, taking care to ease my way down so as not to wake the sleeping vek'tag if she wasn't already shuffling about, ready to hitch herself to the wagon for the day. Or come to testing. Whichever.

"Well, if it isn't little Erith No-Name." Her voice was unmistakable and filled with wicked amusement. She referenced my lack of parentage with all the glee in Sovar. All of it. Some poor child in the Carved Caves would be without their morning dose of glee because Merin Nemy had stolen it all just to be a snot to one of her lessers. It was a normal thing for her.

"It is," I said, resuming a normal pace down the stairs. "I'm up early so I can be tested for magical talent. I assume you're up early because you've got a hard day of pulling wagons ahead of you?" I didn't make a face at all as I said it, just let it drop, deadpan. "Because if so, you're certainly wearing the right dress for it."

I could feel her anger even if I hadn't seen her face across the crowded room. Everyone else had the good sense to be sleeping at this hour, though one person did stir in the corner. "At least I have more than one dress. And walls around my dwelling."

"Why, Merin, we live in the same dwelling," I said, walking at a leisurely pace toward the stairs down to the first floor. "The only difference is that my part of it has a view and yours does not." I cast a look at her over my shoulder. "Also, your dress has vek'tag dung in it." I pretended to peer closer. "Oh, I'm sorry, that's just you. My mistake."

"I don't know why you're bothering to get up," Merin said, standing, outraged, from her place at the table. Her hands ran self-consciously to her dress and she smoothed it, as though she could use the magic she hoped she had in her hands to transform it into a prettier one, one I hadn't just insulted and made her feel bad about. "Everyone knows that low-bred trash have no magical talent."

"Yet every year they turn out all the children for testing regardless," I said, pausing at the top of the stairs. I was within a few feet of escaping her, but this exchange was going far more in my favor than it usually did. I realized it was because Merin was bereft of an audience to point and laugh at me, jeering as they took her side. Alone, with no one to find her snottiness amusing, she had less impact. "But I suppose Merin Nemy knows something that the Sovereign's best do not." I cupped my hands around my mouth. "Quickly! Tell the Tribunal that this year's testing is to be canceled as Merin Nemy knows better than the Sovereign's wizards and healers that there is no magical talent to be found in the Back Deep!" I let my hands fall to my sides, not touching my dress, as I gave her what I can only describe as my evil smile. "You realize though that if what you say is true, then you have no chance of magical talent, either?"

"I'm not like you," Merin sniffed, her hands coming away from the dyed pink fabric of her dress. Even a fool could see it was better made than mine. "I won't be here for long; Daddy says we'll move to the Front Gate, and then I won't have to see your ugly face again, Erith No-name, except when I pass you in the streets and laugh at your two pitiful dresses. You're just a poor, bossy little parentless waif who thinks she's a princess." She cracked a mean-spirited grin.

"I'm sure it's lovely to have a daddy who does everything for you," I said, letting my irritation mask the sting of her words. I felt sick in my heart, in my gut. "And won't he be disappointed in a few years when you're wearing the exact same dresses—dyed brighter but the same size as they are now so you can show off ample flesh when you become a harlot." I broadened my own mean grin, now hollow, and disappeared behind the stairs, running down them before I could hear her reply. She was sputtering in rage, but I had no doubt she'd come up with something artful sooner or later.

I pushed aside the cloth door to the dwelling and felt my feet land in the soft, impressionable dirt on the street. I looked to either side and saw only minimal activity. There were a few torches burning here and there, leaving spots in my vision. I preferred the natural luminescence of the ceiling phosphors, but sometimes there was a need for more lighting. Guards carried torches down the street, merchants worked by lamplight. Even though the city's patron was Yartraak, the God of Darkness, concessions had to be made in order to get things done.

I took in a sharp breath of cool air, catching the scent of Sovar; the manure gatherer clearly had not been by yet this morning, and the whole place stunk more than it usually did. I still felt the jab of pain in my gut, that raw combination of nerves and humiliation. The truth was that I was far more likely to become a harlot than Merin Nemy ever was. She had a father with some money and the possibility of advancement, which was an uncommon thing in Sovar.

People lived and died in the same structures, took over the jobs of their fathers and mothers, never moving more than a few hundred yards their entire lives. Their paths were set; mine was not. I had no path, save for what the Sovereignty bid me do. No apprenticeship waited for me, and should I fail to find a husband—something I had little interest in at this point, all my peers being dullards interested only in sport and jokes about feces—

desperation might set in when the day came that I was no longer a ward of the Sovereign. I knew older girls who had done it, and they certainly dressed better than I did.

I trod down the street, Merin's stupid words, her stupid point, and her stupid being right echoing in my mind. I hated that. My parents had died when I was too young to remember; being a ward of the Sovereign was not something that afforded one an excess of status. It mostly led to all the dead-end places you might imagine in a city in a cave.

I passed two workmen leveling out the street with a plow, trying to smooth over the surface where the vek'tag-drawn carts had left deep ruts in the clay. It didn't look particularly easy, but it was work, and that was something that men jumped upon when they could find it. The workmen grunted, already sweating and looking exhausted even at such an early hour. I didn't care to think about how they'd be feeling by the time the day ended.

They kept on, though, knowing that if an overseer came past and caught them not doing their assigned task, it'd likely be a trip to the Depths for them. Sloth was not tolerated on the Sovereignty's work details. I cringed for them as one of them moaned in pain, and kept walking, avoiding the newly upturned clay for the mess it would leave on my shoes. The workers' backs were bent, their eyes downcast. Instinctively, I lowered mine likewise as I passed.

I wandered into a back alley behind my hovel. It wasn't the safest of places, in retrospect, but who was to stop me? No one, that was who. No one commented when I came in late, no one said anything when I left early, not even Theratas Gruhm. I had been told that a Sovereignty overseer would check in on me twice per year to make certain I was still doing all right, but I hadn't seen him in well over an annum.

I put my back against the hardened mud wall of the dwelling and stared at the one directly opposite. The cut textures of the wall were rough like a stone, but they'd been carelessly sculpted by workmen like the ones I'd passed minutes earlier. All the houses in Sovar were built by the Sovereign's men, by his grace. And they'd been standing since long before I was born.

I heard the ruffle of cloth as a drapery was pulled back. It was the entry to one of the doors across the street, and a man stepped out. I caught sight of him as he let the drape fall back into place, and I recognized that his clothes were of the very finest and dreadfully dull. The absence of color meant he hadn't dyed them, which likely meant he was not from Sovar. Here in the lowers, we dyed everything, including our hair.

He wore robes, white and plain, covering his breeches, with something that looked like a scarf with strange writing upon it around his neck. He snugged a cloak over it and his head before I caught much sight of it. His hair was something straight out of Sovar, however, dyed a bright red. I saw it just before it disappeared beneath the cowl. He didn't look particularly tall, but he was thin, and he looked more than a little worn. His boots were clean and well kept, as if he didn't walk in them often, and made of a strange material that I didn't get a good look at before he began to walk away. He started to go the way I had come, and I blurted something out before I had a chance to stay myself.

"You shouldn't go that way," I said, "as they're smoothing the road." He looked back at me in surprise, and I realized he hadn't known that I was there. "You'll get your boots messy."

The man paused and cocked his head at me then let out a short, sharp breath that was clearly amusement and just short of a laugh. "You say that with all confidence, as though you were commanding me and not offering me warning."

I blinked and felt myself try to retreat, bumping into the wall. It wouldn't do to upset a man from Saekaj, if in fact he was one; the hair was a bit of a mystery. "I ... I didn't mean to—"

"It's quite all right," he said, soothing, holding up a hand to stay my protest. "I only meant that you speak with an unusual aura of command for your age." He smiled slightly. "It's quite ... imperious, actually. I don't know that there's any sweeter way to say it." He bowed his head. "Your warning is well appreciated. Consider it heeded." He reversed his course and walked back my way, tipping his head to me in salute as he passed. "Thank you for your kindness."

"You're welcome," I said and cast a look back at the door from which he had entered the alley. It was the home that had only one family on the third floor. I was young, but I knew enough to put it together. I looked back at him and caught him giving me a slight smile as he vanished around the corner.

*

I lurked in the alley until the appointed hour. I wasn't sure why I had bothered to rise early, other than to get the last of the stew before anyone else did. A gnawing hunger was our lot most of the time in the Back Deep, so I counted myself lucky to have evaded it this morning. I stood with my back against the wall in the alley, trying to tuck myself into the shadows while I thought.

I had hoped so hard for this day, hoped that it would be the day that would allow me to ascend from the depths I lived in. There was little to care for in my circumstances, and if I were told at the morning's testing to pack my few items and be in Saekaj by the afternoon, I wouldn't have thought twice before doing it. I wouldn't have much to pack, either, since all my personal belongings could be carried in the flimsy old spider-silk rucksack that I carried on my back most days. All the possessions I'd ever had of even a little value had been stolen except for the clothes. Only a truly vile person would steal clothes. Even common thieves even had too much pride to do that.

I wondered what kind of life a girl who tested for magic would live. Would it be some beautiful academy with stone-carved grounds, with mushroom patches and bean sprouts growing in the areas outside the windows? I saw it that way in my mind, comparing it to the administration building that was just near the tunnel road leading up to Saekaj. It might be even more glorious than that, for all I knew.

Of course it didn't matter, I told myself, trying to manage my hopes, because I wasn't magical in any way. I told myself over and over that I wasn't special, I was just another poor orphan of Sovar, one of the millions, and I'd be here until the day I died. I'd seen the testings before, just as Merin had. Thousands of girls and boys from the slums lined up in a row, and nearly none got out. Some from the areas nearer the gate sometimes, but never from the Back Deep.

There was no magic in the Back Deep.

No, it was best to realize that my days would be spent here, finding some trade—of greater or lesser virtue, I supposed—and possibly a husband, if I could find one tolerable enough, and then working my days away at my endeavors until I passed. Then I would be carted off to the Depths to be composted, denied a place among the dead of Saekaj in the Halls of the Honored. As for all born in Sovar, that was my path.

I walked with the certainty of failure through the streets, now growing crowded. The testing was held in a square near the guard barracks, a squat, oblong structure that was filled to the brimming with surly men who had no homes of their own and not enough leisure for the hours they worked. Or so Theratas Gruhm had said, and I believed him.

A few of the guards were standing outside the gates as I approached the square. A platform had been placed in the middle of it, a stage constructed solely for the purpose of the testing. A few nervous workmen waited nearby, hesitant in their lethargy because they had no task set before them but dismantling the stage once the proceedings were finished. Their discomfort was palpable, the idleness they had always been taught to fear clearly unnerving them now that they were forced into it. Most stood at attention, ramrod stiff, worse than the soldiers lurking near the barracks gates to keep watch on the crowd. One was laughing and having a good sport of it, like he was in on a joke that none of the rest of them had got. I supposed that was true, because only he was at ease realizing that he wasn't going to be punished for his idleness this day. The rest of them were so conditioned that they couldn't see their way through it.

At that moment, I was reminded of all of us in Sovar—a deep thought for a twelve-year-old. I realized that none of us had gotten the joke, though, as that fellow had.

The square was glum, though a few happy cries of children playing could be heard. These were drowned out moments later by the hissed demands of their parents that they line up. And, oh, there was a line. There always was, and part of me felt like cursing myself for showing up later rather than earlier. I had originally planned to be here far sooner, but my mind had been distracted thanks to stupid Merin Remy. I slipped into the back of the line and saw her already ahead of me. I felt a slight satisfaction as I realized she was wearing a different dress than the one I'd seen her in this morning.

I tried to make myself invisible, waiting as was mandated. I couldn't see the stage, set high as it was, except to realize there was a table upon it and three cloaked figures behind it. "League monitors," I heard the mother in front of me whisper as she dug her fingers into the shoulders of her darling boy. He looked chub of cheek and somewhat frightened, and I knew in a blink he lived by the Front Gate, not in the Back Deep. His mother's dress sold it for me; it was only minimally dyed. I looked down at my bright red attire. At least it was pretty, if a little threadbare.

There was no grand announcement when things began; that was saved for the rare occasions when they found someone of talent. I knew this from years past. The smell of the dark elves bunched in a knot around me was oppressive, and the line had continued to fill in behind me before it began moving right on time. There was a pushy father guiding his youth behind me, a man for whom compulsive sniffing seemed to be a habit. I listened to him with much amusement as I heard him try to control this; the line was not a fine-smelling place, that much was certain. His sighs and the occasional gagging noise that followed his forgetful lapses before a heavy breath were all that sustained me during the boring wait.

It felt like the day had all but slipped away before the line drew in sight of the steps leading to the stage. I knew this to be untrue, having been to prior ceremonies and found them to last only until midday, but standing there waiting for them to tell you that you were just as ordinary as the rest of the children of Sovar—or more so—was discomfiting. And boring. Mostly boring.

Merin Remy crossed the stage in a most perfunctory manner, and I saw her disappointment, unable to be disguised, when the men in black cloaks said something to her that was not well received. She curtsied in a way that made me a little sick then shuffled herself off the stage. I realized that she had been lying to me, that secretly she had hoped that she did have the talent. It seems so obvious now, but to my twelve-year-old self it came as a shock.

It was with great discomfort that I came up to the stage steps a few moments later. I had vowed after seeing Merin Remy curtsy that I would do no such thing. Everyone else was so deferential to these men on this stage, even as they delivered the same pronouncements over and over—"You're not special, now go away." I already knew I wasn't special, living the way I did. I didn't need a panel of three to drive that point home to me in words; Sovar had made it abundantly clear every day that I lived there.

"Name?" asked a guard overseer next to the stage steps.

"Erith," I said, and pushed my chin up.

He looked at me through the slotted visor of his metal helm. "Family name?"

"None," I said with a shrug like I didn't care.

He grunted in acknowledgment and then looked up to the stage. A phalanx of his fellow guards had formed up behind the stage. I wasn't sure why; I'd never seen the populace get out of line at one of these things. It wasn't like the food riots we'd had a decade earlier. I had no memory of those, just whispers from the adults in my dwelling when they thought I wasn't listening. One did not talk about rebellions in Sovar. It was a fast way to find yourself in the Depths.

"All right," the guardsman said as the chub-cheeked lad in front of me crossed the stage after being told (probably for the first time) he wasn't special, either. I could see his shoulders slump as he wended his way back to mommy. I saw her clasp him in a tight hug, but I saw the disappointment in her eyes. And yes, I smiled a little. Because I'm mean, I suppose.

"Come on, then," the guard said, and tapped me lightly between the shoulders with a gauntleted hand. It hurt a touch, but it was more shocking than anything, and I fired a look back at him that he didn't even see; he was already looking at the person behind me, the kid with the sniffing father. I resisted the urge to slap the stupid helm off the guardsman's head as I climbed the steps and made my way to stand in front of the table with the three cloaked figures behind it.

I let out a sigh when I got there, loud, obvious, annoyed. "Are we done here?"

I heard a deep quiet settle over the figures behind the table for just a moment before the one at the center spoke. "You just arrived."

"Yes, and now I'm wondering if I can leave," I said, suppressing just the littlest bit of nerves. It was really like talking back to a teacher. What was the worst that could happen? I remembered what a beat too late as I looked off the stage and caught sight of the metal stocks with a shriveled body locked into the one at the farthest end. Oh, right. That. My irritation faded, replaced by a swell of fear as I realized I needed to scale myself back somewhat. Just to be safe, I decided to tread on this side of the line from outright rude. It was difficult, I'm not going to lie.

The cowled heads shifted, looking from one to another, exchanging glances I couldn't see. Finally a gruff voice from the one on the end said, "You don't believe you have magical talent?"

I paused, trying to figure out how to phrase my reply. I took in the gathered crowd, separate from the line, of all the children who had already waited and been found unworthy. "I'm from the Back Deep," I said. "And no, I don't think much magical talent pools down there."

The voice of the man at the left interrupted with a low laugh. "And how are you to know where the depths of magic pool? Do you feel the subtle embrace of the spellcaster's power in the night, entwining with your life's essence?"

"Probably not," I said, and pointed at the crowd, "and neither do any of these other people, apparently."

"Lord of Darkness, what a tongue on this one," the man on the right said in utter disgust. "The disrespect—"

"She's said nothing disrespectful that I've noticed," said the cloaked figure in the center. "She just isn't bowing and kowtowing the way the others have." I could see the faint outline of his cowl move, as he turned to the figure on the right. "Is your ego so weak that you cannot handle the prospect of a twelve-year-old doing anything less than kissing your arse?"

"She is impudent," came the response of the one on the left, much calmer than the one at the right.

"She's imperious," came the voice of the one in the center, rife with unhidden amusement. "And I sense the stir of magic in her."

There was a low hiss from the one on the right. "Dahveed—"

"Shhhh," the one in the center—Dahveed—said. "Can you not feel it?"

The one on the right held his tongue for a moment. "Yes," he said with greatest reluctance. "Of course."

Dahveed turned left and received a nod in acknowledgment. "So," he said after a moment. "It would appear some magical talent does run down the slopes to the Back Deep." I could sense his smile as he said it. "The magic burns a fire in you, young lass, and gives your tongue license to wag with excess energy." He stood, taking care to tuck his cowl so as not to reveal his face, then motioned for the guard at the bottom of the stage steps who had taken my name and swatted me as I passed. "Her name?"

"Erith," the guard said, almost falling over himself to run up the stairs. "Erith ... Nameless," he said, as though uncertain. The man on the right side of the table made a sound and lowered his head to rest in one hand.

"An orphan," Dahveed said, standing. "Very good. We haven't had one of those in ages, have we?" He looked to the left and right.

"Ages," the one on the left agreed.

"I consider it a hopeful sign," Dahveed said. "Very well, young Erith. It would appear you will learn the delicate art of magics."

I had followed the whole exchange, which had taken only a few seconds, but I still scarcely believed it. "Uh ... all right."

The man named Dahveed laughed at this. "A fitting response for one so skeptical." He stepped from behind the table and a low rumble came from the crowd. "Let us announce this, shall we?" He moved to stand beside me, and when he looked down, I caught a glimpse of the outline of his thin face. "Let us give the people the good news."

I didn't say anything, and the men on the left and right of the table both stepped up to the edge with Dahveed. "On this day," called the man on the left out over the crowd, "we find from the darkness of Sovar one of talent. Her name is Erith, a child of the Sovereign." I grimaced slightly at this, having never met the Sovereign and knowing full well I was not one of his bastards. They lived in the palace in Saekaj. "She will be taken into the care of the Leagues, given training, and raised to a position fitting one of her ability." I heard the man on the right make a guttural sound of deepest disgust at this, but I ignored him. "The Sovereign thanks the people of Sovar for their gift of Erith." I could feel him pausing where he would have said a last name, and he omitted the next part, where he would have thanked my parents. "When you see this child next, she will be a woman grown, and a caster of spells, a weaver of incantations, and exalted among men and women for this rarest of talents. Praise be to the Sovereign!"

There was a muttered wave of exaltation at that, a little muted, but when the man repeated it again, it grew in force as the shock dissipated, and the third time it required not even his suggestion before the words "PRAISE BE TO THE SOVEREIGN" echoed through the cavern.

I watched the faces below the stage, staring up at me with all trace of boredom gone. I caught sight of the workers waiting to the side of the stage, waiting to tear it down. They were watching with rapt attention, their nervousness gone and replaced by wonder. The faces in front of me gazed up in awe, smiles on some, expressions overcome with amazement and even—happiness?

"Erith," I heard a faint voice say, at a normal volume, and I looked to see the stoop-backed figure of Theratas Gruhm, the old man who shared my dwelling. He said my name again, and it was picked up by another voice, then another until it spread over the crowd in a low chant. "Erith. Erith. ERITH. ERITH!"

It rose in pitch and intensity until it was a near-deafening roar, and I felt a hand land on my shoulder and looked up to see the face of the man who had been called Dahveed, still shrouded in the shadow of his cowl.

"You should bow," he said, "to your people."

It took me a moment, but I did. I stooped low, a curtsy that was more sincere than any I would have made to the men on stage if I'd been compelled. My heart was light, and as I dipped down and lowered my head, I caught sight of Dahveed's boots, barely visible under the hem of his cloak. They were stitched, made of a foreign material, and a fine shade one didn't see in the depths of Sovar. They were undoubtedly the property of a man who was unused to treading the muddy paths of the Back Deep, but still as clean as they had been when I'd seen them walk out of the dwelling across the alley from mine.

*

You do not know Sovar. Not her depths, not her darkness, and not her wicked ways and subtle temptations. But then, once, I did not know magic. I did not know the power of an incantation, the ability to heal. These things have changed. All things change, as I have seen in the years since I have left the Back Deep. And one can hope that maybe—just maybe—someday Sovar will change as well.

THIEVING WAYS

Note: This tale takes place around the same time as Chapter 16 of **Defender: The Sanctuary Series, Volume One** and several months before Aisling joins Sanctuary.

One

"I want to steal the Red Destiny of Saekaj."

The sole lamp above the stone bar in the establishment that was known on the streets of Sovar as simply "The Unnamed" cast the man across from Aisling in a dim light. His name was Xemlinan Eres, but so far as she knew, everyone in Sovar simply called him Xem. His eyes glistened as he stared at her, waiting to see what response his confession would stir.

For her part, Aisling took a long, slow breath and picked up the small glass in front of her on the stone bar. It sat unevenly, the natural curves of the surface tipping it slightly to the left. She had grown up with wooden furniture, real wood, but that was a rare commodity in Sovar. She lifted the dirty, smoky glass, tinged by what looked like carbon scoring. The strong aroma of the Reikonosian whiskey, an illegal import, stung her as she breathed it in, burning her nasal passages as if she had poured it into them instead of between her lips. It lit a fire in her, and she tipped it back before clacking the glass back on the bar as she felt the whiskey burn all the way down. The sound of the glass touching the stone echoed in the Unnamed, and Aisling let out a breath that stung just a little—the way she liked it when she took a drink of something. "I'm listening," she said.

"No one's ever tried before," Xem said, his face alight with something more than the glow of the lamp. "It's a slap right to the face of the Tribunal—"

"Because we want to slap the face of the ruling body of Saekaj Sovar while we're still living here in the city," Aisling said with cool detachment as she held up the empty glass for Xem to see.

"Sorry," he said, and hastily reached for the bottle nearby to refill it. He spilled just a little while he was doing so, and Aisling watched it splash on the bar. Xem was usually such a steady hand, too. "Think of it, Ais. It's a gem twice the size of your head."

She didn't even blink. "And it'd be an ill replacement for losing said head if we were caught." She tossed back her drink. "You're talking about breaking into the Sovereign's palace—"

"Which he's not even using at present," Xem interrupted.

"True, the Sovereign has been away for the last century," Aisling agreed, "but he's been replaced by a triad of men so thoroughly loathsome that the only policy they've come up with that hasn't incited hopelessness or anger in the masses is the Exodus Proclamation that opened the gates, allowing hundreds of thousands of our people to leave the city and their strangling grip."

"And that is why we should slap them in the face!" Xem was nearly triumphant about the whole thing.

Aisling felt herself disengaging from the situation. "This is starting to sound personal," she said and began to turn to get off the short, flimsy stool she was resting atop. "I don't do personal jobs."

"It's not personal," Xem said, shaking his head. He came around the bar in a hurry, catching her before she could retreat. Well, that wasn't entirely true; she moved slowly, giving him the opportunity to do so. *No one can catch me if I don't want them to,* she thought with a deep satisfaction. "I want the Destiny. Have you ever seen it?" Xem's face was hopeful.

"No," Aisling lied.

"It's a mammoth ruby," Xem said, his eyes widening as though he were seeing it in front of him right now, in the moment. "Its worth is incalculable—"

"I'm not so keen on objects of incalculable value, either," Aisling said, making a clumsy move to slip past him. He caught her, just as she planned for him to. "Too hard to fence afterward, which leaves you stuck holding them when the guards find you."

"Thirty million gold pieces," Xem said, his eyes dancing.

Aisling hesitated, thinking it over. "Awfully low, if it's a ruby twice the size of my head."

"But that's the beauty," Xem said, and took a ragged breath, "we're done once the ruby is delivered. We take our gold and leave Saekaj Sovar out the main gate. I've arranged transportation with an elven wizard just outside the borders. All we need do is clear through some guardsmen—"

"With our thirty million gold pieces," Aisling said dryly, "which I'm sure won't attract any attention." She rolled her eyes, but in truth she was just playing him, waiting for him to remove her mental objections.

"It'll only be seven and a half million each," Xem said, "split four ways."

"Oh, well that solves the problem of transporting them entirely," she said.

"I know, it's still a lot," he agreed, "but there's a convoy leaving a week from now, and I've arranged for us to join it, along with six wagons to haul our take. It's going to Aloakna, and it'll also be bearing gold in the shipment, and thus we'll pass unnoticed."

Aisling pulled her arm away. "So you've covered the escape," she said, playing it to be almost grudging, like she wasn't expecting that. "Do you have a plan to steal the Red Destiny, then? Or just an extraordinarily detailed idea for fleeing afterward?"

Xem grinned. "I have a plan for that as well. And if I may be a bit immodest—"

"Hardly a first for you, Xem."

"It may in fact be one of my most genius," he said, ignoring her quip.

Two

Aisling slunk through the door, letting her feet make little to no noise. He was on her a moment after she walked in anyway, catching her from behind and wrapping his hands around her leather top. She let out a small gasp, feigning surprise, and felt his lips on her neck, eliciting a giggle before he set her down and allowed her to spin about.

There was only a dim lamp in the corner of the small room for light, but it was plenty enough to see him by. His dark blue skin almost faded against the dim clay walls, and his face was alight with mischief—just the way she liked it. "Norenn," she murmured and met his lips as they came down to hers. "How goes it?" she asked coyly, slipping out of his arms.

"'How goes it?'" Norenn Vard's voice was laced through with disbelief. "Don't be so sly; you know I'm waiting to hear."

"Waiting to hear what?" she asked in feigned ignorance. In her quest to become a better thief, she was getting quite good at acting. She gave him her best innocent look, and she could tell by his smile that she had done well.

"Very good," he said with a slow nod, "but if you don't tell me, I'm going to—"

"Going to what?" she asked. The facade broke and a smile slipping out.

"I don't know," he said with a grin of his own, "but it will be appropriately proportional to the discomfort you're causing me."

"The meeting went well," she said. The summons had come unexpectedly, an offer to meet in the wee hours of the morning, after the Unnamed had closed. "He had a … proposal for us."

Norenn tapped his vek'tag silk shoe against the floor. "I know that. One is not summoned to the Unnamed in the middle of the night without good cause. What was the proposal?"

"Something … grand," she pronounced, strolling behind the stone chair that had been carved out of the floor. "Something to build a reputation on."

"Oh," Norenn said with more than a little disappointment. "I don't care for those kind of jobs; building a reputation in Sovar is the fastest way to ensure that your personal story ends with, 'And he spent the rest of his life digging ore and spreading manure in the Depths.'"

"He has an excellent escape plan," she said with assurance. In truth, she had to suppress the excitement quivering in the pit of her stomach. "It's a sound scheme."

"But big, if it's a reputation builder," Norenn said and turned away. "How big?"

"The Red Destiny of Saekaj," Aisling replied, waiting to see Norenn's reaction.

"I hope you told him no," Norenn said, the reaction coming more swiftly—and far more soundly—than she had anticipated.

"Of course I didn't tell him no," she replied. "I listened to the basics of the plan, judged it on its merits, and—"

"No," Norenn said, slumping against the wall. "No, no, no."

"Why not?" She crept toward him, laying a hand upon his vek'tag silk vest. It was far nicer than most clothing found in Sovar, an ill-gotten gain from one of their previous jobs.

"Because even if he has a masterful plan to steal it," Norenn said, "the kind of reaction that this will prompt from the Sovereignty will be enormous, bringing so much fury upon us, on Sovar—"

"The escape plan," Aisling said, "includes leaving afterward. Possibly forever."

Norenn's mouth opened slightly. "Leave Sovar?"

She slipped the hand up from his vest to his face, feeling the smooth fabric against her palm turn to stubble from the day's beard growth. "You've always said you didn't want to spend your whole life here."

"Yes, I figured I'd travel when I was older, once my fortune was made," Norenn said, opening his eyes to look down on her with reproach.

"This is a chance to make your fortune," Aisling said, smiling sweetly at him. "Seven and a half million gold pieces each. Fifteen million total, and we leave Saekaj Sovar afterward. We can return someday if we want, or put the money on deposit with a bank in Reikonos, Aloakna, Termina, wherever, and just ... travel. Be free."

"Ugh," Norenn said. "'One last job,' is that it?"

"Yes," she said, and gave him a soft kiss on the cheek. "One final score, and we can be done if we want. Or not. All we have to do is give up Sovar for a while, which is ..." she looked around at the hovel they lived in, a one-room stone cave in in the side alley caves off the main chamber, "...

let's face it, is no real sacrifice."

"This is home to me," Norenn said stiffly. "I know it's not much of one to you—"

"Home for me is wherever you are," Aisling said, and she tried to say it with sincerity. She smiled to give it extra weight, but Norenn laughed a little even so. "I'm serious," she said. "I'll go wherever you are. But this is a chance to make it big and just go—"

"I've been a thief for a long time, my dear," Norenn said and pulled away from her. "I know what it means when one of our kind says, 'One last job, one final score.'" He sat in the chair again and laid his arms down on the stiff stone rests. "It means they're getting greedy, that their sense of careful planning has been overtaken by a serious lust for gold. And you know what?" He didn't wait for her to answer. "It always goes wrong, that last score. They flub it somehow—the mark catches on, they screw up in the planning stage, they overestimate their skill or they just leave too much to chance." He sat up in the chair. "So when I hear you say, 'one last job,' it makes me nervous."

"It's a good plan," she said, kneeling in front of him at the chair. "It's solid. Yes, there's risk, but no more than any other job we've done, and with a much higher reward." She rested a head on his knee. "You know I don't care about the reward from 'one last big job'—"

"I know," he said, and she thought she caught some bitter irony in there.

"—but this one is worth it. Even the mid-levelers in Saekaj don't make seven and a half million gold pieces in their whole lives. It's a fortune the like of which most of our people could never even imagine."

"Yes, well I'm imagining it right now," Norenn said sourly, "and I'm imagining what will come after it—namely the entirety of the Sovereignty's guards. This isn't just calling down the force of Sovar's militia, this is asking for the Sovereign's personal guards and the army to come after you. So you'd better be sure the plan is good enough to deal with that. Good enough to handle everything that will come out of it—and I'm talking about house-to-house searches by irritated guardsmen, fearful of the Tribunal's boot landing on the back of their necks." He stood abruptly. "This is ... so dangerous."

"Thievery carries the eventual death penalty in Sovar," she said, and stood to join him with a slight smile. "The Depths being the means by which they carry it out. How much worse could the penalty be than for any act of thievery we would carry out on any other day?"

"It's not the penalty," Norenn said, "it's the effort they'll put in to catching us. And it will be enormous."

"Which is why we leave," she said. "Slip the grasp of the Sovereignty when we're finished." She smiled. "It's a good plan."

Norenn sighed, and she sensed his capitulation. "I feel absolutely mad for even considering this."

"But you're in?" she asked with a smile.

"I will listen," he said, a small concession, but one that she knew meant that she had him. "To Xem. I want to hear it from him."

"Good," she said coolly, catching the distinctive, sharp aroma of his vek'tag silk vest as she rubbed her cheek against it. "He wanted to discuss it with you in any case, along with our other partner. I set it up for tomorrow."

"You were awfully presumptive," Norenn said with a hint of stiffness. "How did you know I would go along?"

"I presumed I could persuade you," she said, still rubbing her cheek against his chest, against the silk.

"And if your arguments failed?"

She let her hand sink lower.

"Ah," he said as she leaned up to kiss him. "It would appear that Xem is not the only one with a sound plan."

Three

Xemlinan stood before the three of them—Aisling, Norenn, and Leneyh Ousck. Leneyh was extremely slight, smaller even than Aisling, and prim, as if she'd been born to Saekaj, though Aisling rather suspected she was a practiced imposter. Her navy skin and undyed white hair served to mark her as a member of the upper class, and her monochromatic clothing reinforced the image. She was stunning, though, even Ais had to admit, especially after the third time she caught Norenn's eyes wandering to the hem of the woman's dress. She gave him a gentle tug and he brought his eyes front again.

"Any questions?" Xem asked. They sat in the back room of the Unnamed, a couple of lamps burning their dim light out over a small storage room stacked nearly to the ceiling with glass bottles.

"When do we do it?" Leneyh asked, her small, piercing eyes almost languid in their motion. *No lady of Saekaj would be as comfortable down here as she is*, Aisling thought. *No proper one, anyway.*

"In a week," Xem said, the small parchment he'd made drawings on still hanging from his fingers. He'd used charcoal to sketch the vault, laying it out step by step. Ais had scarcely breathed as Norenn watched intently. Finally, around step five, he'd nodded, and she could see the first signs of approval from him. That had allowed her to breathe a little easier. "It should give us plenty of time to get our hands on the few things we need—appropriate attire, enough rope—"

"Why are we doing this?" Norenn asked, his fingers touching his chin pensively.

"Beg pardon?" Xemlinan asked, slightly taken aback.

"Why are we doing this?" Norenn asked again.

Xem smiled a little patronizingly. "For the money, of course."

"There are easier jobs," Norenn said.

"Name five," Xem replied with a ready smile, looking between Leneyh and Aisling for support.

"The Bank of Sovar, The House of Grimrath Tordor, The Bank of Saekaj, the Eristant Museum of Art, the Lowerquarter Storehouse," Norenn said, rattling them off one by one. "Every one of them filled with goods that are easily fenced, save for Grimrath's and the Museum, and with the exception of the banks, less likely to draw the ire of every guard in the entire Sovereignty."

"But I have a buyer for the Red Destiny right now," Xem said, recovering with a smoothly delivered answer. "So that trumps gold, paintings, artifacts or easily movable food stores."

"And you have verified their ability to pay?" Norenn asked, fingers still upon his chin.

"I have," Xem said, and there was the first hint of tightness in his voice. "So, if I may continue—"

"Why?" Norenn asked again.

"Norenn," Aisling said in a low hiss. His rudeness in pressing the matter was beginning to raise her ire.

"Why are we doing this particular job? I want an answer," Norenn said. "The plan looks sound, seems sound, and sounds wonderful. Yet I hear a certain quiver in his voice as he speaks it all, something that leads me to believe that he is doing this for more than just the money. What is it, Xemlinan? Did the Tribunal cross you in some way?"

Norenn's manner of speaking to Xem was entirely familiar, and Aisling knew they'd crossed paths before in their careers in the Sovar underworld. Still, it felt rude, and she was on the verge of telling him to shut up when Xemlinan spoke. "You are correct," Xem said, nodding with great reluctance, his face a mask. "I have a grudge, you might say, against not the Tribunal itself, but the head of it, Dagonath Shrawn."

"You do pick the enemies," Norenn said. "Dagonath Shrawn also heads the most powerful house in Saekaj."

"And is uniquely placed to throw an inordinate amount of grief in the faces of us lesser beings who might happen to cross his path," Xem said. "Which is what happened in my case."

"So you want to steal the Red Destiny to spite him," Norenn said and crossed his arms. "To put a thumb in his eye by stealing the Sovereign's greatest treasure from the Grand Palace of Saekaj."

"As head of the Tribunal, Dagonath is in charge of the palace whilst the Sovereign continues his extended … absence," Xem said with great discomfort around mentioning the Sovereign. "Should it disappear, I imagine a great, slicing blade will land upon the neck of the House of

Shrawn upon the Sovereign's inevitable return. So it is effectively doing two things at once—financing my retirement and allowing me the petty satisfaction of knowing I've cast a great boulder over a cliff's edge while Dagonath Shrawn is wringing his hands helplessly below."

"So we come to the truth," Norenn said, arms still folded. "A revenge job and one last score to boot." He lowered his head. "There are so very many ways in which this could come back horribly upon us."

"I'd ask you to name five, but I expect you'd rattle them off in short order," Xem said with something approaching apprehension. "Do you find flaw with the plan?"

"I don't know the subject of the robbery well enough to find flaws," Norenn said, and to Aisling's ear it was almost plaintive. "That is what worries me."

"I know the palace," Aisling said, drawing a startled look from Xem. She swallowed heavily. "I was raised in Saekaj—"

"You?" Leneyh said in sneering disbelief.

"The dresses I left behind in the wardrobe of my parents' house when I left are much prettier and more stately than anything you've ever worn," Aisling said with a smile. "Xem's reading of the security at a palace ball is on the mark, and he has identified one of the surest ways to pass it." She cast a look at Norenn. "The plan is sound, save for perhaps the vault security; I cannot speak to that."

"Fine," Norenn said, shaking his head. "But would it not be better to steal it in a less guarded location, such as when it is on display—"

"And protected by the entirety of a legion of the Saekaj militia?" Xem shook his head. "No, the vault is where it is weakest, because they are overconfident in their security measures."

Norenn sat back, looking again at the parchment. "It's not hard to see why. It's an impressive bit of security."

"Which can be contravened through careful planning, though admittedly not easily," Xem said. "The timing is crucial and will require the full commitment of all involved." He leaned forward and Aisling saw him hold his breath. "I need to know if you're in or out, right now."

Norenn looked sidelong to Aisling. She didn't dare look back, keeping her gaze off him for a full count of ten seconds before turning to give him a cool stare in reply. "Very well," Norenn said at last, after a space that felt like an infinity. "I am in. I only hope I do not end up regretting this."

"So do we all," Xem said with a dry amusement. "We have one week to plan, prepare, to get all of the necessary items and ready ourselves." He held up the parchment upon which he'd drawn, and touched it to the flame of a nearby lamp until the corner caught fire. "After that we are committed." He looked up at them as it began to burn, the flames spreading up the page. "Enjoy this week, fitful and busy as it may be." He smiled as he cast it aside, tossing it into a metal pail just to his right as the fire took over and the parchment shriveled and blackened. "For if all goes according to plan, it will be your last in Sovar, possibly ever."

Four

The window squeaked just slightly when she forced it. She'd left it unlocked when last she'd been here, but that was no guarantee that one of the maids hadn't come along behind her and fixed that for her. It had been a long time since last she'd been home, plenty of time for someone to discover what she'd done. She breathed a sigh of relief when it opened after she applied pressure, only a slight squeak heralding her arrival at her childhood home. *Just the way I want it,* she thought. *Not a sign, not a whisper, nothing to tell them I've been here save for an item missing that they surely won't notice.*

She climbed in, slipping quietly through the gap, careful not to make a sound as she did so. She'd had to climb up to the second floor using spikes that affixed to her palms, and it required all her upper body strength to do so. The advantage was that few thieves bothered to, and even fewer would chance doing so on an estate in Saekaj; the security was too heavy, and the guards at the gates of Saekaj barred anyone who wasn't a citizen of the upper city from passing without cause.

Her feet landed on the floor with the barest of sounds. She wore climbing spikes over her cloth shoes but had removed them when she reached the roof and placed them back in the pouch on her belt. Now she padded across the soft rug in near-silence to the wardrobe that took up half the wall. She opened it slowly, eliciting another squeak that she hoped wasn't really as loud as it sounded to her. She reached into her belt and pulled a small vial of grease. She put some on a bare finger and ran it across the hinges of the wardrobe before opening it further. This time it swung open in silence, and she wiped her finger on a cloth she kept for just such a purpose before putting her glove back on. *Must remember to put some on the window as well, in case I ever have to return via this route again.*

She looked into the open wardrobe, squinting into the darkness to survey the dresses held within. They were fine, all shades of black and white, stunning and—she hoped—still in fashion among the Saekaj elite. *For this job, less stunning is better. Something that blends, something that covers all, doesn't catch anyone's attention ... something with a full skirt that touches the ground.*

She selected a larger gown, one that covered her shoulders, in black, a color that had been out of favor when last she'd been to a ball. *Hopefully that means it's back in favor now, it's been so long.* It wasn't form fitting, which was another advantage; she knew she had grown since last she'd worn it, and it would need to be adjusted—*the less it has to be adjusted, the better off I'll be.*

"Come to sell that for money?" The voice cracked behind her like something had been whipped past her ear even though, she realized after a moment, it had been low and quiet, almost inaudible. "In need of some fast coin in order to continue to survive in Sovar?" Aisling turned to see her mother standing at the doorway, her face more lined than it should have been, given that she was not even a century old.

"No," Aisling said, suppressing her shock. "I actually need it for a ball."

"Don't lie," her mother said with a hissing sigh that revealed a disappointment fathoms deeper than Aisling wanted to plumb. "It insults us both."

"I'm not lying," Aisling said, numbly. "I need it for a ball."

"You little fool," her mother said with deep disgust, "there are no balls in Sovar. No singing, no music; it is the Sovereign's decree, and you well know—"

"It's not in Sovar," Aisling said, crumpling the material of the dress she'd selected in her glove.

"Then you're trading on your family name for ill purpose," her mother said, touching a hand to her face. "I don't want to know about it. Your father …" her voice trailed off.

"Yes?" Aisling stared at her, not moving.

"He rarely speaks of you, he can so little hide his disappointment," she said finally.

"I'm sure I'll tear up about that later," Aisling said, running her gloved hand over the material. She felt nothing, just the sensation awareness of running her fingers over something soft. *Rather like living in this house all those years.* "Goodbye, Mother." She started to leave, carrying the gown over her shoulder.

"You could use the door," her mother said, making a sound of disapproval so profound it might have been rooted in the Depths.

"I could," Aisling said, sitting on the window's sill in preparation to spin around and put her legs through. "I could enter through the door, leave through the door, sleep in that bed," she waved a hand at the enormous, four-poster monstrosity in the corner. "I could take my meals in the dining room with you and father, attend all the social events that you always took pleasure in filling my schedule with, strive for the highest marks my expensive tutors would give me whilst impressing them with my intellect and memory." She took a breath of the stale air of the bedroom then leaned out the window and caught the scent of the cave air, the potency of it. "But then I'd still be living in your house, under your roof, and subject to you and your rules." She pulled her knees to her chest and then spun on the sill, dropping to the roof's ledge just below the window. She stood and turned, ducking to look back into the window. "Which is why I used the window to come claim what I wanted, and why I use it now to leave."

"Like a common thief," her mother said with utter disgust. "I thought I had raised you better."

"I'm an uncommon thief, actually," Aisling said. "Farewell, Mother. I don't expect we'll meet again."

"That would be too much to hope for, with you in the state you are," her mother said, anchored to the spot near the door. "Gallivanting around the rooftop of the manor house, sneaking in—why, I should have the guards revoke your citizenship to Saekaj, leave you trapped in Sovar like the ungrateful rat you are."

Aisling managed a half-shrug. "You presume that I only have the one passbook to get through the gates."

Her mother looked scandalized. "You ... you ... forger!"

Aisling shrugged again, whole this time. "I left my real name behind a long time ago," she said with a wicked little smile. "Imagine my embarrassment at the idea that someone in Sovar might think me related to *you*."

"There are worse things than being related to one of the noblest houses of Saekaj," her mother sniffed.

"I don't see much noble about your house," Aisling said and began to slide the window shut. "Don't forget to lock this behind me." She cradled the gown under her arm, taking care not to let its hem touch the dirty rooftop. "You wouldn't want to have me ever come back, after all."

With that, she felt the gentle click of the window slide into place and turned, crossing the roof at a whisper-quiet pace. She looked back only once, and it was because she had to turn to drop off the ledge to the ground below, anyway. Or so she told herself as she vanished beneath the edge. The last thing she saw before she dropped to the ground below was her mother's face, pressed almost to the window, watching her daughter disappear into the darkness.

Five

The night of the ball, they entered Saekaj by separate paths, Aisling and Xem through the main gate at different times, and Norenn through an old smuggling tunnel that he was well acquainted with. The logbook at the guard station would have record of their passage, which was why Aisling used false papers whenever she traveled.

She approached the Grand Palace of Saekaj after the ball was already in full swing. Because the roads to the Grand Palace were necessarily narrow due to the construction of manors on either side of the major thoroughfare toward that end of the cavern, only members the highest-ranked houses in Saekaj were permitted to take carriages to balls held at the Grand Palace. All but the twelve most noble houses in the present order were forced to walk, leading those invited from the outer edges of the nobility to have to travel some distance. Aisling saw a woman with terribly punishing heels on her shoes and knew that she was from middling nobility at best but trying desperately to look more important than she was.

The whole of Saekaj was laid out so that one's status could be measured by proximity to the Grand Palace, where the Sovereign resided during more august days. With the Sovereign's exodus had gone the game of currying favor, wherein the great noble houses of Saekaj vied for his approbation, with obvious results. Possession of manor houses shifted according to whoever was in the Sovereign's good graces, the largest and most luxurious manors being closest to the Grand Palace. That system, what her elders called "The Shuffle" had been suspended for her almost a century. *For as the Sovereign has been gone.* She sniffed and walked along, thinking that in reality The Shuffle had never truly ended, just ceased being a game that resulted in one trading up or down with one's manor house.

Aisling passed the largest of the manors on her left as she approached the Grand Palace gates in a small flow of pedestrian traffic, attendees and servants alike. It was the House of Shrawn, a stone manor carved into the wall of the chamber with a facade so grand that it left no doubt that it was the most impressive one of its kind in Saekaj. Gargoyles and other statuary of incredible craftsmanship dotted the flat roof, decorating the opulent home of the head of the Tribunal that ruled in the Sovereign's absence. Guards with swords lurked just inside the gate of Shrawn's manor, watching the partygoers pass by with smoky, uncaring eyes.

Aisling turned her attention back to the gates of the Sovereign's palace as she passed a guard and flashed an embossed, gold-papered invitation at him. It flickered and an illusion of the Sovereign's seal appeared, an enchantment designed to make the invitation impossible to forge. Aisling imagined some enchanter in the Tribunal's employ was sitting, even now, in a room in Saekaj, maintaining said illusion on several hundred invitations, having not eaten, slept, nor drunk since they went out. She suspected the one in her hand was not a forgery, though she was uncertain who Madam Y. Urnetagroth was, having never heard the name before.

The Grand Palace of Saekaj lived up to its billing. The upper floors of the structure could be seen from the main gates, so long as they were open, and allowed almost anyone, even those from Sovar, to get a glimpse without entering Saekaj proper. The entire facade was gilded, and shone in the light of half a hundred torches mounted on the outside. Aisling had always thought it being so well lit was a curious dichotomy, what with the Sovereign's professed loathing of the light. If anyone noticed it as hypocrisy, nothing was ever said. She shrugged inwardly; for all she knew, it had been added in the last few years, long after the Sovereign's exodus.

The palace was at least ten stories in height, the facade fading into the back cave wall after a hundred feet or more of stone-carved building. It was the work of great craftsmen who had worked the rock for years to hew the palace out of what had once been entirely a solid wall of the cavern. A small, dark moat encircled the structure, a drawbridge allowing passage over it. Torches had been set out, and the moat shimmered with their reflections.

She passed under the enormous portico that was there to protect against the occasional cave drip. A single noble was disembarking, not from a carriage but from a palanquin carried by four strong servants. The passenger was female and she carried herself arrogantly, as though all she was seeing displeased her.

It was Leneyh, Aisling realized after only a moment, violating the rules of protocol in spirit if not in letter by having herself carted up to the entry of the Grand Palace in such a way. No one said anything, at least not loudly, the muttered whispers of the dark elves around her confirming Aisling's suspicion that on the next grand occasion, several others would be trying the same thing. *Too bad I won't be here to see the fracas that results,* she thought. *Oh, wait—no, it's not; I always hated these things.*

She ascended the small number of steps to enter the main foyer of the Grand Palace. It was an entrance truly befitting a Sovereign's residence, and she paused for just a beat to take in its beauty. It was warm and inviting, the way she imagined a palace in the upper world would look, with wood covering every square inch of the floors and elaborate carvings covering the walls.

There was a distinct dearth of stone sculpture, which was perceived to be a lower form of art given the abundance of stone available for carving and the relative scarcity of wood. The entire place reeked of opulence and of another smell, that of pines and oaks, distinct scents she had learned in her childhood while sniffing the furniture in her parents' house—and which she hadn't smelled since, save for on the occasional thieving job. She had to admit, of all the things she missed from trading down, wooden furniture was near the top of the list.

"Madam Urnetagroth," Xemlinan said, sweeping in to tuck his arm through the crook of her elbow. "It is such a pleasure to see you this night."

"And you as well," she said with a nod. "Xemlinan Eres." She smiled at him and Xem returned the smile. She looked around, wondering if anyone had heard her. It didn't matter, ultimately; Xem was well known in Saekaj circles and had a legitimate invitation in his own name.

"May I show you to the refreshments?" Xem asked, guiding her toward the buffet in the far corner of the next room without even waiting for her to answer. She stifled her irritation; it was customary to follow a man's every suggestion in the male-dominated society of Saekaj Sovar, but it was something that she would never get used to or enjoy.

"You may," she agreed. They took their time making their way across the packed ballroom. She looked back and could no longer see the entrance to the foyer through the crowd. The ball was teeming with elves, and Dagonath Shrawn had plainly had to hold it in the Grand Palace simply in order to accommodate all the guests.

The black and white hues of the women's dresses were stark in the low light of the room. Even with the torches burning, the ball was a dim affair, absolutely at odds with the bright lighting outside. An unsubtle way, perhaps, of drawing the attention of the uninvited to the palace, of saying,

"Look at us!" *Crass. Ordinary, at least in Saekaj.*

"I trust you had no difficulty getting here?" Xem said in a low voice, low enough that it could not be heard over the quiet strains of chamber music echoing in the ballroom.

"None at all," Aisling replied, letting the corners of her mouth tug up in an entirely fake smile, a well-practiced one that drew on her still-burgeoning acting skills. The nervous tension was gnawing at her stomach, and every step felt surreal, as though she had not slept in days. The affair seemed entirely too loud, the conversations and the music blaring in her ears despite being relatively quiet compared to a Sovar street on market day. *Sincerity,* she thought. *Be delighted to be here, like these vapid whores.* "And you?"

"I tread these paths regularly, so I suspect the guards are quite used to me by now." Xem tightened his grasp upon her elbow. "Your gown is really quite lovely, and very much in vogue."

Ais smiled. "The women of Saekaj are nothing if not predictable."

Xem frowned. "Beg pardon?"

"Nothing," Aisling said with a light shake of her head. Her hair was done up for the occasion, knotted about her head in a bun that was both tasteful and designed to keep it out of her face during crucial moments. "We meet Norenn by the table."

Guests were already swarming the buffet table, a thousand hands picking delicacies off the surface. The smell of rich food wafted off it, filling her nostrils with delightful aromas that replaced some of the heavy clouds of perfume she'd walked through to get there. It was nothing less than a feast of hors d'oeuvres, all manner of imported food and local delicacies—vegetables grown on the surface, pastries baked of flour imported from the Plains of Perdamun, fresh catch teleported in by wizards from Aloakna and not the bony offerings of the Great Sea that rested several hundred feet beneath them. There were sweets aplenty, and Aisling snagged a sugared loaf of bread as she dipped past the table.

An enclave of fat nobles were already having their way with the buffet, reflecting the belief that the best way to show status was to expand one's girth. She shook her head at the thought, having been told more than once by her mother that a fat girl was a girl quickly married. She looked down at her waist, which had always been thin but had grown thinner after two years in Sovar, and wondered if she'd ever even want to grow fat, even after she had all the money she could imagine.

"It's a bit like a knife fight in the Back Deep here," Norenn's voice said from behind them, causing Aisling to turn in surprise. He was there, darting furtive looks toward the head of the room, where a recessed segment of the wall held an alcove that was so shrouded in shadow nothing could be seen within it. "This entire room is so self-obsessed that I doubt a single one of them has noticed me since I got here."

"Best to keep it that way," Xem said, finally turning Aisling's elbow loose. She hadn't minded the gentle pressure; it was certainly more gentle than most of the boys who had asked her to dance or give them her company at these sort of things. "Only one of us should garner any attention tonight, and it's not you, I or her," he said with a nod to Aisling.

"Quite right," Norenn said with a quick nod. "Still, few enough guards are posted at the exits, very light numbers overall." He nodded quickly at the dark alcove. "That makes me nervous, though. I don't think anyone will notice us so long as there's not someone hiding in there watching the room."

Xem chuckled. "There's no one in there."

"No?" Norenn said with a raised eyebrow. "Care to bet your life on it?"

"He's right," Aisling said quickly. "It's the Sovereign's alcove. That's why it's so dark. No one would dare be in there without him."

"All right, then," Norenn said, but she could see by his upright posture that he was still nervous. "I suppose we're just waiting until the signal."

There was a loud noise across the hall, toward the foyer, and the three of them froze. "I think that was it," Aisling said.

"Quite right," Xemlinan agreed, and nodded to Norenn. "Shall we be off?"

"Lead on," Norenn said, keeping his voice low.

"Madam," Xem said, clutching Aisling's arm once more. She suppressed the desire to make an annoyed sound, realizing that Xem was simply doing it because an unattached woman was likely to be grasped by another man. Still, she couldn't shake the annoyance entirely.

They cut their way through the crowd as a hush began to fall. They headed toward the alcove at the top of the room, and farther and farther from the entry and the foyer. Raised voices crackled through the ballroom, over the heads of hundreds of people who had stopped and begun to shuffle nervously, listening to the unfolding drama.

"Leneyh Ousck, you have no manners at all!" The voice lashed over the entire room, a stinging rebuke landing on its intended victim.

Xem chuckled almost soundlessly at Aisling's elbow. "I knew Lady Glasherney was a sure target."

"Better to have no manners than no looks," came Leneyh's reply, echoing across the cavernous room. "For I may choose to learn manners at any time."

A swell of delight ran through the crowd, and Aisling tried to act as though she were paying attention. Xem had slowed their pace, trying not to be obvious about their motion, even while the rest of the crowd was solely focused on the dispute at the far side of the room. They shuffled sideways, pretending to be jockeying for better position, all the while sidling toward the far wall, right where the attention of everyone in the crowd squarely wasn't.

"One guard moving off the door," Norenn said under his breath.

"Two to go," Xem muttered. "Leneyh should escalate things ... now."

"Don't think I don't see you there, chuckling with insufferable satisfaction at this, Lady Hrenshaa," Leneyh's voice came over the crowd, drawing a few gasps. "I suppose you think this display of disgusting vulgarity by Lady Glasherney is simply marvelous, given your proclivity for live shows of the most ribald kind."

Aisling felt herself cringe inwardly. Leneyh was going to need every piece of gold to escape the city after this night. "She's really earning her money," she said quietly.

The three of them reached the wall just between the Sovereign's alcove and the far door, now left with one guard to keep watch on it. He was not keeping careful watch, however, instead craning his neck to see where his compatriots were cutting their way through the crowd, gently shoving toward the center where Leneyh and her targets continued their verbal jousting.

"I have my doubts that this one will leave," Norenn said nervously, placing his back squarely against the wall.

"Oh, he'll leave," Xem said, but his grip tightened on Aisling's elbow, belying his confidence. "There is, after all, one last thing to be done ..."

"She hit me!" Leneyh's shocked voice came over the crowd. Aisling could not see the fracas by now, but the simple and soul-deep conviction with which Leneyh had spoken the words made her wonder for a fraction of a second if it was, in fact, true. *Master actress, that one. I could learn a thing or two from her.*

The crowd began to teem with life, people scrambling for better position, standing on chairs. She saw a group of men in the far corner standing on a table in full armor, doubtless dark knights from some brigade held high in esteem, noble sons of noble men who were now standing around watching women argue with each other at the society event of the season.

"And that's three." Xem's grip on Aisling's arm relaxed. "Let's go," he said as she caught sight of the last guard breaking away from the door, sprinting into the now-milling crowd, where some shoving was going on closer to the Sovereign's alcove.

They made their way along the wall, the wood paneling touching her through her dress. She happened to glance back as they reached the door, looking into the darkness of the Sovereign's alcove. It was completely enshrouded in shadow, an absolute refuge of darkness in the middle of the semi-lighted room. She had looked into it a thousand times, just like every girl her age, wondering about the gazes of fear that older women at these balls cast at it, women with clear memories of things that had happened in the days before the Tribunal ran the Sovereignty.

"Come on," Xem said, a note of excitement infusing his voice as he reached the door. "Hurry."

She bent and did her work quickly, two picks from her hair tripping the tumblers within seconds; she'd learned how to pick this type of lock in her parents' house what felt like ages ago. "In we go," she whispered as Xem held the door for her.

Norenn entered first and Aisling followed, taking one last look back at the crowd, which was still alive with people pushing forward, trying to see the disturbance at the far end of the chamber. Not a soul looked back at them as she disappeared into the door. Her last look before she entered the shadowed corridor was of the Sovereign's alcove, still practically radiating darkness, and then Xemlinan followed behind her and shut the door.

Six

The hall was dim but her eyes adjusted quickly, a faint, musty smell of unused corridors replacing that of sweating bodies and the exquisite buffet. The long, dark hallway before them was a quiet affair, pillars every few hundred feet stretching off into the distance. They could either go right or straight ahead, following the hallway into the distant darkness.

"This way," Xem murmured and started forward. She found she missed the gentle pressure of his hand at her elbow and looked to Norenn for reassurance. He smiled at her, faintly, but she could sense in him nerves similar to the ones tickling at her belly. Hers were born of mostly excitement, though; his, she suspected, were more rooted in fear.

They tiptoed down the hall, Xem making more noise than she would have thought a master thief of his reputation would make. There were enormous arches supported by columns, the entire palace a monument to the opulence of the Sovereign's excesses. She heard a faint noise in the distance and knew there were guards in these hallways. She took a quick breath and exhaled, trying to listen to determine their direction. After a moment she realized they were far off, not nearly close enough to be worrying about.

The palace hallways became a catacomb of twists and turns as they reached another branch. This was all Xemlinan's part of things, knowing where to go, and he seemed to be going by memory. The smell of must was still heavy in the air as they passed countless doors, and she realized after a brief pause that Xem was counting doors and corridors.

"You're certain you know where we're going?" Norenn asked.

"This is the single greatest job of my life," Xem answered a moment later. "Do you think I would foul it by failing to memorize the map of the palace?" He turned and gave Norenn a rakish grin. "I have spent every night for the last year reading the map before going to bed and repeating the same sequence in my mind. One hundred eighty paces, corridor left. Forty-nine paces, corridor right. Straight ahead for two hundred paces, even as it curves." He held out a hand to indicate how the corridor curved downward, following the natural caves that it had been built into. "Ignore the next two lefts, then take the right-hand door." He said it with a sing-song quality, as though he had set it to music only he could hear.

"Far be it from me to doubt you," Norenn said, almost apologetic—at least for Norenn. "It is a maze down here, though."

"It is," Xem agreed, turning back to the path. "It's designed that way. In the days of the Sovereign, only the trusted would know the plan for their segment of the palace. The guard quarters required their own map, the servant quarters got their own, the bastards—" he looked back at them, "the Sovereign's children, I mean, they got their own wing with their own attendants and kitchens. Very few people were allowed the run of the entire palace, allowed to know the entirety of it. Fewer still was the number allowed to know anything at all about the layout of the Sovereign's private quarters. It took me the better part of two years to put the right combination of former servants together in order to get an accurate map." Xem slowed as the corridor straightened out again. "Right hand door ahead," he said with quiet glee.

Aisling reached the double door a couple paces behind Xem, who halted at the handle and made a grand display of it to her. She rolled her eyes and sank down next to it, pins once again out of her hair. She picked it in seconds, shaking her head at the ease. "There are tougher tumblers in Sovar."

"It's all old," Xem said, giving them a reassuring look to squelch the one of panic that had appeared on Norenn's features. "The Sovereign doesn't set any stock by innovations, you well know. In addition, this palace has only been maintained in the years since he's left, not renovated or changed in any way." He smiled faintly. "I think they were afraid if he noticed any change, it'd be their heads for doing something he didn't command. Right," he turned the handle and opened the door, "in we go."

"Right," came a voice from just inside as a spear jutted out of the open door and poked Xemlinan in the gut, harshly enough to elicit a grunt. "In you come, and out you'll go … to the Depths, criminals."

Seven

Aisling drew the dagger from her sleeve and brought it down on the arm that held the spear at Xem's belly before the door had a chance to open any further. The blade was honed to a fine edge and she slipped it into the gap between the arm plates at the guard's elbow. She buried the knife in the meat, dragging the spear out of Xem's belly before it could burrow any deeper. Her attack left the arm limp and dangling.

Norenn hit his side of the double door with his shoulder, knocking it open. An armored figure went down behind it, Aisling realized as she caught sight of a gauntlet flailing just behind the paneled door.

She followed Norenn and whirled around the still semi-closed door to bring her other blade across the throat of a man still crying out in pain and clutching his half-severed arm. His eyes grew wide as she slipped her dagger between his gorget and the strap of his helm, and took care to dodge to the side as the spurt of blood narrowly missed her dress.

Aisling turned to see how Norenn was doing, but the guard he'd hit with the door was already down, his helm off. Norenn held a short, blunt club that he'd concealed up his sleeve. He brought it down on the guard's skull again and again.

"I think he's dead," Xem said quietly, with a slight grunt of pain.

"How are you?" Aisling said as her foe slumped to the ground, still hemorrhaging blood from his neck.

"Shallow wound," he said, poking at his own midsection. "Hurts, but I think I'll be fine." He took off his jacket with utmost care to reveal a dark stain on his white shirt. "I'll need to bandage myself up and wear my jacket buttoned, but I think I'll be all right to escape." He eyed Norenn, who was splattered head to toe in blood. "You, on the other hand …"

"Eh?" Norenn looked down at himself, then to Aisling, and his jaw locked tight. "How am I supposed to make it back through the party looking like this? I look like I've butchered a vek'tag."

"You did go after that guard with some enthusiasm," Aisling said.

"First thing's first," Xem said, looking around the room. "We have to get the Red Destiny."

"Are you joking?" Norenn said, and extended his arms wide. His once-white shirt was colored with obvious spots of blood. "How am I supposed to get out of the palace looking like this without drawing attention to myself? Let alone with the Red Destiny of Saekaj."

"A minor problem, nothing more," Xemlinan said, glancing back before returning to his survey of the room. "This, on the other hand ..."

The room was a sprawling almost-square with a two-story high ceiling. It was stone all the way through, with arches and columns around the perimeter and what looked like a balcony overhead with a chandelier hanging in the middle.

A domed structure was sticking out of the floor. It glinted in the low light of the single torch lit in a sconce on the wall, dull metal catching the glimmer of faint light. Aisling took a step out from beneath the balcony, just a step behind Xem. "This is it," he breathed. "The vault."

"Yeah," Norenn agreed, surveying the area with a nervous air. He looked back at Aisling. She tried to smile at him but found her gaze drawn back to the vault. "Let's get this over with so we can solve that trifling 'problem' of getting out of here."

"Agreed," Xem said, kneeling next to the domed lid. "Ais, would you care to try the first method?"

"Sure," she said and looked to her left. Hidden in the shadows under the balcony was a recessed doorway. She closed in on the door and realized it was, in fact, open, and the light caught the glint of something within, then another something, then another. "It's definitely activated now," she said, halting just before the aperture.

The door was crossed by blades, jutting out of the walls as the tunnel beyond led into a spiral and down, toward the bottom of the vault some hundred feet below, she knew. She glanced back at the dome in the center of the room; the Red Destiny of Saekaj was hidden within, at the bottom of the vaulted chamber, and the tunnel walk down was the preferred method for retrieving it. The vaulted dome was usually used for something else entirely: feeding the predators that guarded the treasure.

She ran a finger over the flat edge of a blade that barred her entry into the door. Three others blocked her within the first inch, and more were just past that, an impenetrable maze of blades skewering the center of the tunnel leading down, knitted so tight that even a gnome wouldn't be able to pass between them. She looked to her right and saw the hole where a key would go, then found another matching hole to the left of the door. She frowned and jogged back to the fallen guards.

"They won't have keys," Xem said, looking up at her as she passed where he and Norenn were working on the vault. "Those are kept by only four people, and it requires at least two of them to open it."

"I'm just checking," she said as she stripped one of the guards down and searched him. She made a small stack of their belongings off to the side—armor, clothing, weapons, and added the gold from each of their purses to her own after checking to make certain Xem was not watching. It took only a moment, after all.

Once she had confirmed that neither had a key save for the one that unlocked the chamber door, she made her way back to the keyholes and prodded them with her pins. Neither responded favorably, and she smelled something strange as she worked, something that caused a tingle to run across her skin.

After a few minutes she felt her skin grow warm from the exertion and stripped off her gown, laying it carefully in the corner. She was left in her underclothes, and caught a sidelong look from Norenn that she waved off with a simple, "It was always going to have to come off anyway." He gave her a partial glare, the sort of thing he did when he knew she was right but didn't care to admit it. It wasn't as though she were nude under it; she had a pair of dressing shorts and a lace-strapped undershirt, after all. That and a length of thin wire spider web filament that was wrapped around each of her arms and threaded around her abdomen. She unwrapped it quickly, casting it off to the side in a coil.

She prodded at the right-hand lock for another few minutes before coming to a conclusion. Something was blocking her ability to turn it, something she could not see or identify, something that was wholly unlike anything she'd ever seen on a lock before. She probed again, and was rebuffed, the tumbler failing to even move slightly. She withdrew the pin and turned, looking to Xem. "This seems to be completely immune to lock picking."

"Uh huh," Xem said, focused on the dome. "Just as well," he said, adjusting the small metal cone he was holding up to his ear. The other end was firmly placed against the vault dome, and Norenn stood next to him, almost smiling. Almost. "I think we've ... got it!" He let out a small gasp of triumph and then slid the wheel atop the vault around once more until a click echoed through the whole chamber. Xem pulled himself and the cup up as Norenn scrambled to open the dome. He pulled on it once, then twice, only stirring it a bit until Xemlinan joined him. Together they lifted it up. It opened with a squeak, revealing hinges hidden under the dome that allowed it to be lifted to a roughly ninety-degree angle to the floor. Aisling threw a locking pin into place to secure it open, and the three of them peered over the edge into the darkness below.

"We'll need a torch," Xem proclaimed before walking over to a wall sconce and pulling an unlit one off. He made his way to the sole burning torch, lit his upon it, then threaded through the support columns back to the vault. He leaned over and peered in, and Aisling followed after him.

There was a powerful smell coming from the hole, something foul and most rotten. "The hounds?" she asked, covering her nose at the scent.

"Surely," Xem said, trying to look into the darkness. "They'll be down there, guarding the approaches." He chuckled. "I can believe no one thought of this before." Light caught a glistening web only a few feet below them and he cocked his head. "That's a ... rather large spider web."

"Oh ..." Norenn groaned. Ais shifted her gaze to him. His eyes were closed, a sick look upon his face.

"What?" she asked.

"How do you know that there are hounds guarding the treasure?" Norenn asked Xem, still looking a bit ill.

"They bring fresh meat down here every day," Xem said weakly. "They've been known to throw undesirables down here, according to my source." Now Xem looked sick as well, and Aisling turned back over the edge, staring at the webs below. The torch caught the light of another set of webs, just below that, and another further down.

"Oh," she said, now feeling more than a little sick herself. "Not hounds. The meat's not for dogs at all."

"No," Norenn agreed. "Hounds would be near useless in guarding a vault of this sort. But a lovely breed of giant spiders, on the other hand ..."

Eight

"What now?" Norenn asked, glancing at Xem.

"Not sure," came the reply.

"I'll go down," Aisling said, staring at the first wave of webbing. She was oddly calm, certain that somehow down there with the Red Destiny lay her own, and she wanted—no, needed—to go down into those depths, even with the added danger.

"Madness," Norenn said, giving her the look. The smell coming from the vault was nearly overwhelming, a sickening aura of digested meat excreted, and other meat wrapped in webbing for later. "You don't know how big those things are."

"As big as a vek'tag?" Aisling asked with faint amusement.

"Probably not," Norenn said. "Vek'tag are tame and they stick to mushrooms, roots and insects. These are probably Depths spiders, about a quarter of the size of a vek'tag, more maneuverable and poisonous. They're one of the leading causes of prisoner death."

"Only *one* of the leading causes?" Xem asked weakly.

"Yes," Norenn said with some tension. "The number one cause is being killed by overseers or exhaustion."

"I can handle spiders," Aisling said, feeling the chill return now that she had remained stationary for a few minutes. "I've got a knife."

"Poisonous spiders," Norenn added, staring flatly at her.

She didn't look away as she answered. "I'll be all right."

"Let's go quickly. Better to get this done with as soon as possible," Xem said, retrieving the rope from near her discarded gown. He flung it up and over the edge of the balcony above, threading it through the stone railing. Once he'd retrieved that end, he tossed it up and through the chandelier.

"You're sure the chandelier will support her weight?" Norenn asked. He was chewing his lower lip now, Aisling saw.

"Yes," Xem replied, catching the last of the coil. There was over a hundred feet of slack remaining now, even after he'd threaded it through both the railing above and the chandelier and tied it off on one of the columns. He dipped low and tied it around Aisling's ankles, giving her a smile as he did so. "Norenn," he said, and motioned for Norenn to stand at the point where he'd laid the slack before threading it over the chandelier. "Hold it tight while I guide her down into the vault." Norenn nodded once as Aisling lay down on the cold stone floor to avoid having her legs jerked from beneath her.

Norenn began to very slowly pull the filament, levering her legs from the ground, followed by her entire body. The blood rushed to her head and the upside-down sensation flooded her. *Good thing I didn't eat before this.* She felt extreme disorientation, her head swimming, until she got hold of it. They had practiced this several times in the last week, and it always ended the same way—she had only minutes to retrieve the Red Destiny before she passed out. Which would mean the loss of the Red Destiny of Saekaj as well.

"All right," Xem said, guiding her with hands placed firmly on her hips. He shuffled her sideways and she felt the motion of the rope as Xem pulled it along the edge of the chandelier to better position her under the vault. "Are you ready?" He let betray the slightest edge of concern.

"I'm ready," she said then looked down into the dark. "Torch?"

"Ah," Xem said, stooping to retrieve one he'd left burning on the ground. He handed it to her then tossed another down into the vault. She watched it land on the spider webbing below, where it burned its way through after a few seconds, then fell to the next level of webbing below, where it halted for a few more seconds. The first level of webbing sagged and fell with the hole the flames had produced, and she stared down, eyes trying to discern where the bottom was.

"Long way down," Xem said, patting her once. She looked over at him then past him to Norenn, who held the rope, his arms locked into place and a look of slight strain beneath his mask of concern.

"Let's do this," Aisling said and drew her knife with her free hand. She kept the torch in the other, holding it above her head. Her vision flashed, leaving a spot in front of her eyes when she turned her head to look. She felt the rope begin to move, lowering her into the dark chamber below.

She heard the straining of the chandelier as she eased down a few feet. She dangled, rotating slowly in a circle. The neck of the vault tapered down to an hourglass shape. She fell toward the center slowly, a grain of sand in the middle of it. The spider webs just below her were flapping in the breeze coming from up top. Her skin was chilled, the sweat from her earlier labors now drying in the cold air. She kept a tight grip on the knife and the torch and tried to control the spin of her body as she continued to be lowered.

The walls were a honeycomb of holes, as though the entire vault had been built with a careful structure of small arches surrounding the center. There was a creak above from the chandelier that got her to look up without thinking. Neither Norenn nor Xemlinan were visible now, both working on the rope to keep her suspended.

"All right down there?" Norenn shouted, loudly enough that his voice echoed down to her.

"I'm fine," she shouted back, hoping that the vault was sealed off enough that no one would hear them bellowing back and forth.

She continued to dangle as the rope lowered her, the shift in perspective between up and down still not something she was used to. With every sway of the rope she felt dizzier, the first hints that her body would not be capable of handling her position forever. She gripped the knife more tightly, readjusting her blade so that she could strike more easily with it. Still there was no sign of anything but discarded spider webs, burned by the torch that Xem had thrown down.

She was approaching the center of the hourglass and her eyes spied movement below. Something anchored onto the wall shifted at the neck of the funnel. She could feel it watching her, even though she couldn't see the eyes. It made noise, a subtle sound of legs moving that sounded like the cracking of dry straw. Something moved, and she saw a bone fall from beneath the legs of the spider, the image burning itself into her mind as it fell below.

She readied the knife as she drew closer to the spider, holding it back to strike as she passed. She paused after a moment's thought and thrust the torch out instead. The spider moved back of its own accord, easing away from her as she passed. *Oh, no,* she thought as her upper body passed into the narrowest part of the vault, *my legs are going to go right past him ...*

There was a clicking sound and she folded at her midsection, thrusting the torch up as she passed. It hit the spider as it started to lance out at her, a pincer hitting the fire. It emitted a hissing sound almost like a scream. A moment passed and her legs were beyond the spider, out of its reach.

"Let us know when you get to the bottom!" Xem shouted from above. She could see him up there now, leaning over. Her descent had slowed somewhat, probably because he wasn't helping to lower her any longer.

She didn't answer, turning instead to look down. Something glistened in the light below her, something on a pedestal that was emerging from the shadows as she came down. It glowed red when she waved the torch, the light reflecting back at her from it.

"There you are," she whispered to herself. It was only a few feet away now. "Slow me down!" she shouted back up top, and saw Xem wave over the vault top. Her descent became a crawl for the last few feet down as she moved toward it, the glimmering object that stood in the middle of the centered pedestal.

The Red Destiny of Saekaj.

It had a multiplicity of facets, it was so large. It was the size of a melon she had once seen at a feast. She called out, "Stop!" and a moment later, she halted, dangling only a foot above the pedestal. With a calming breath, she held herself still, gently swaying in the air. She sheathed her dagger then laid the torch across the pedestal's side. It was wide enough that there was a half-foot of space on each side of the Red Destiny.

She grasped the gemstone in her hands, feeling the weight of it. It was certainly heavy, though not as heavy as she would have expected. She tucked it under one arm, making certain it was secure in the crook of her elbow before grabbing the torch back off the pedestal and tucking it into the hand that held the Red Destiny securely against her side.

"Now comes the fun part," she said, and tried to blink the spots out of her eyes. These, she feared, were not from the light of the torch but rather from being upside down for so long. "Start bringing me up!" she called, and Xem waved at her. There was motion above, even after he disappeared beyond the lip of the vault, barely visible through the narrowing walls at the center. "Oh, crap."

She could see motion above, off to the side of the entry hole. The spiders seemed to be operating at the periphery of her view. *Gonna have to wait until I'm past the hourglass center to see what's waiting, I suppose. Either that or tell Xem to stop pulling and give me some idea of what I'm going to be dealing with. Well, that's the smart way, but it'll sure slow us down ...*

She approached the narrow center of the room, the walls tapering close on either side, squeezing tight around her. She crunched her abdomen, feeling the soreness from trying to defy gravity. The blood rushed out of her head. She felt nauseated and dizzy, and forced a breath to try and regain her head. She kept the torch at the ready, the Red Destiny squeezed tightly into her side, cradled closer than she would have any squalling infant, that was certain.

She passed the neck of the hourglass and the hissing came from her left. She swung the torch and connected with something, the fire illuminating pincers and legs as a spider was knocked back. It fell into one of the arched holes and Aisling smiled. *One down.*

When she looked up her smile vanished.

"It's getting harder to pull you up!" came Xem's voice from above. He was not visible at the opening of the vault, which meant he was probably pulling. *Alarming, since I'm not moving very fast.*

She held the torch aloft and her fears were confirmed. There were a dozen spiders above her, working threads, spinning them across the gaps that had been created earlier when they'd tossed the torch down. Black, eight-legged figures spun their way down lines, and she could see two spinning their webs around the line of filament she was dangling on. Whatever they had done was producing resistance, keeping the rope from rising as quickly as it should have.

Thanks to the light coming from the room above, she could see the faint glint of freshly spun strands. There were so many spiders working around her, though. She wondered if the spiders re-spun these webs every day after the guards threw food down to them. It was a disquieting thought, especially considering the speed with which new, gleaming threads were being knitted above her.

"Throw another torch down!" she called, wondering if Xem would think to ask why before doing it. She prepared herself to dodge whatever he threw. "Careful not to hit my rope!"

Xem appeared at the edge of the vault, torch in hand. "Good gods," he said, loud enough she heard him. "I don't think I can throw it without hitting you. You're too close to that narrowing part of the chamber."

"Dammit," she breathed, and tried to fold herself again, bringing her head up as she pulled her abdomen tight. She took the torch and waved it, causing her body to go into a slow spin. Nausea hit her now, the spin coupled with the still-pooled blood in her head overwhelming. She felt the urge to vomit and suppressed it, instead trying to pick out individual threads of web as she spun then touching the torch to them as she passed. Her upward pace was a crawl, a few inches at a pull, and coming in great, uneven motions. She jerked with each tug of Norenn's efforts, forced upward a few inches and then stopped in a halting motion.

She burned another few threads and saw one of the spiders go swinging past her making that same hissing noise she'd heard earlier. It hit the wall, the fiber anchoring it severed by the flames. It was one of so many, though, and they seemed to be crossing the light above with such frequency she knew it could not be long until she was completely webbed in.

"Throw the torch!" she called out again, lighting another few threads as she dangled past them.

"It will hit you!" Xem said.

"Do it anyway!" She saw it drop and tried to prepare herself. She brought her own torch closer, clutching the Red Destiny to her as the falling torch hit her feet, then tumbled into her leg, tapping her in the head briefly with the unlit end as it fell. "That was close," she muttered as it fell past her. It had dropped several layers of fibers, and she could see the spiders swinging, their support burned free underneath them. The pace of her ascent increased, even with Xem lingering above her rather than rejoining Norenn to help pull her up. She was getting close, only ten feet or so from the lip of the vault, and the spiders were hanging on the walls, well away from her. She heard not even so much as a hiss when she crested the edge.

"Here," Xem said, taking hold of her waist as soon as she was up. He pulled her sideways, dragging her to where she could grab the cold stone floor, rolling the Red Destiny away from the hole. To Xem's credit, he didn't so much as look at it, instead focusing on helping her get to solid ground once more. When she was firmly away from the vault, Xem crossed to the dome and pulled the pin, gently lowering it back into place. "Don't want those things getting out," he said with a smile.

"No, we don't," Aisling agreed. Norenn appeared at her side, and she felt the blood leave her head in a great rush as he helped her upright.

"How are you?" Norenn asked, eyes rimmed with concern.

"A little woozy," she said. "About like the practice runs, maybe a little worse. I'll be ready to go in a few minutes."

"Good," Xemlinan said, stooping next to her. He had the Red Destiny of Saekaj clutched in his hand, a smile wide on his face. "Once we get to the servants quarters, all we need do is leave the palace and we're free."

"Oh, only," Norenn said under his breath. "We only have to leave the most carefully guarded building in Saekaj, that's it."

"Well, you have to admit, it's easier than getting *into* the most carefully guarded building in Saekaj," Xem said with a smirk. "After all, we have an exit."

"Help me up," Aisling said, then staggered to her feet with the help of Xemlinan and Norenn. She felt the unsteadiness working at her, as if her legs were new and weak. She stumbled over to where she had left her clothes and grabbed the gown. She slipped it on, careful to let it fall over her cloth shoes.

They went through the double doors and back into the hallway, following Xem's lead. He steered them back through the curves, and up a slope, murmuring numbers that were in his head as they went. "Forty-five steps and right ..." He stopped before a door. "Here." He looked them over. "Aisling, are you ready?"

She sighed. "Give me a moment." She frowned at him. "And turn around." Xemlinan smiled slyly and complied.

"Are you certain you can do this?" Norenn asked, giving her a worried look.

"I have to," she replied, and bent down to lift her skirt. Norenn knelt before her as she drew it higher and lowered herself slightly. Norenn gave her an uncertain look once more and then placed the Red Destiny of Saekaj squarely between her thighs. She clutched them together tightly. "Although I think it's ironic; my mother cautioned me when I left home that if I was moving to Sovar, I'd have to make my money by opening my legs, not keeping them tightly closed."

Xemlinan let out a muffled laugh, and even Norenn smiled at that. She dropped her skirt and clenched her thighs tight around the surface of the Red Destiny. "You must admit it's a rather ingenious way to smuggle it out. No one would dare to search a noble lady's person in such a manner."

"I'll admit it's ingenious if it works," Aisling said, straining her muscles. They had practiced this with a large stone, but the Red Destiny was surprisingly lighter. "Until then, I'm going to continue to wish we'd gone with the idea of dressing me as a pregnant woman and hiding it in the empty sack."

"Harder to impersonate a pregnant woman's mannerisms than it is to simply walk very, very slowly," Xemlinan said. "Are you ready?"

"As ready as I'll ever get, standing here with what feels like a ton of weight bearing on my legs."

Xem opened the door to the servants' quarters and the three of them filed in. They were empty, of course, the servants all busy at the ball in one form or another. Aisling practiced shifting her eyes down, her hair already knotted atop her head. *Giggle if you can. Look a little furtive, like you've been a naughty little slattern here in the Sovereign's palace. Feed into their notions of why someone would be sneaking around in the servants' passages.*

They filed out into the hallway past the servants quarters, a better-lit passage. "This way," Xem murmured, guiding them toward a clatter that was rising from the kitchens.

They emerged into a wide space, ovens roaring with flames, heating the room. Aisling found it unreasonably warm, like being curled up next to a furnace, and could feel herself starting to sweat. *Not good. Maintain the hold on the Red Destiny.* It was hardly a serious matter as yet, but she felt a deep urging to get out of the kitchen as quickly as possible. The smell of all the rich food was wonderful, but her urgency drove her to avoid so much as glancing at the available dishes.

"Here," Xemlinan said, darting toward a nearby door. Aisling giggled as she followed, aiming for flighty. Xem held it open for them, and she vanished into the dark outside of it with only a single glance back into the kitchen to confirm what she suspected—everyone pretended not to see them go.

Nine

"Not far now," Xemlinan muttered as they stepped out of the door.

"What am I supposed to do now?" Norenn asked, eyes shifting nervously. The blood was apparent when he unbuttoned the jacket, showing it to the two of them. "I may not have drawn attention from the servants, but I can't pass the gate guards like this. They're sure to pick me out."

They had paused just outside the kitchen door, now outside the Grand Palace and back in the main cave of Saekaj, but behind the walls still. The main gate was a few hundred feet away, behind one of the extended wings that jutted out, obscuring their view.

"I have an idea about that," Xem said, and his voice betrayed a hint of tension, "but I don't think you're going to like it."

"What?" Norenn asked, hopeful and suspicious all at once.

"You'll need to look like you've hit someone," Xemlinan explained calmly.

"So you're suggesting we make it look as though we've fought?" Norenn asked, glancing to Aisling. "Won't that draw suspicion?"

"Tremendous amounts of it," Aisling said, wondering what Xem could possibly be getting at. Fights between men at the Sovereign's palace were grounds for an immediate trip to the Depths for at least a month. "The only way you could possibly get away with hitting someone at the Sovereign's party is—" The answer came to her, and she sighed. *Men.* "Ugh."

"Sorry," Xem said, and she could hear the note of apology. "Up to you, but ..."

"Brace against my legs so I don't drop the Red Destiny," Aisling said, and Xem did so to her right.

Norenn pushed in against her left leg, looking a little baffled. "Are you wearing out?"

"No," she said, "I could walk considerably farther. But I don't want to fall when I do this."

"Do what?" Norenn asked.

Aisling smiled at him tightly. "The only thing that's going to allow us to walk out of here with blood on your shirt." She raised her hand, clenched a fist, and punched herself in the nose with everything she had. Spots flashed before her vision and she heard a faint cracking noise.

"What are you doing?" Norenn said, catching her arm as she slumped a little.

"Is my nose bleeding?" she asked, trying to regain concentration enough to check. She ran a hand across her upper lip and found it wet, a warm stickiness spreading. "Okay, good, we're set."

"Oh, gods!" Norenn said, and Xem shushed him. "You expect me to walk out looking like a woman beater?"

"It's socially acceptable," Xem said quietly. "Sad as that is to say. Happens all the time at the Grand Palace."

Norenn said nothing for a moment, his face shrouded in shadow. Aisling watched him, could see the thoughts spinning in his head. "Let's get out of here," he said finally, every word grinding out like it was spit from a mill, the double meaning more than obvious to her ears.

"I couldn't agree more," Xem said, and each of them took one of her arms as they shuffled off.

Ten

There was a small crowd at the gates, dark elves passing through with only the occasional glance from the guards who stood outside, spears at the ready. The three of them shuffled along nonchalantly, avoiding scrutiny by any of the guards they'd run across along the path to the bridge where they crossed the moat. *I suppose it's a normal sight in the Grand Palace to see two men escorting a beaten woman toward the gate.* She seethed inwardly but tried to stifle it. *I'll be away from here soon enough. Not far now.*

"Once we're out of the gate, Leneyh will have a carriage waiting for us in the market," Xem whispered as they neared the gate. "Just a little farther, half a mile at most."

"I'm fine," Aisling said, but in truth her eye was beginning to squint shut and her legs ached almost as badly as her nose. *I can make it. For this fortune, I could carry it back to Sovar between my legs.*

The guards were still, two facing in on the sides of the pillars that held the gate. Two others waited just outside. She could see their arms behind the pillars, a spear jutting upward from one of them.

They crossed the threshold of the gate without fanfare, without anything beyond a stray look from one of the guards who took her in with one glance then promptly returned to staring straight ahead. Aisling felt the pain in her thighs, a low, racking agony that was starting to spread down her legs and up to her back. Her nose was still dripping blood, and she sniffed lightly. She looked right and saw Norenn's shirt, still dotted with blood. No one dared say anything. *Predictable. Sadly predictable.*

"My gods," Xem breathed once they were out of earshot of the guards, halfway down the wall that shielded the front of Dagonath Shrawn's manor from view, "we did it."

"We're not out of the city yet," Norenn said.

"Quite right." Xem was back to stern once more. "But you might consider taking a breath once we're in the carriage."

"Perhaps," Norenn said, glancing at Aisling. "Are you all right?" he asked, his voice lowered.

"I'm fine," she replied, ignoring the aches and pains. The street still carried the faint scent of the perfumes that had been worn by all the ladies who had trod this path, lingering long after they'd passed on to the ball. She smiled, grimacing when a bead of blood slipped between her lips and she tasted the metallic tang of it. "Or I should say I'll be fine once this is done and we're out."

She only just glimpsed Norenn's faint smile. "Where should we go?" he asked.

"Just out for now," she said, the ache in her thighs growing. "Once we're out, we can pick a direction."

"I was thinking of Reikonos," he said, glancing at the nearly empty street around them. "It's well out of the reach of the Sovereignty, and—" he paused, and there was a noise behind them. "What's that?"

"Changing of the guard," Xemlinan said with only a glance back. "Come on, we're only a little ways off—" There was a noise, something sudden and loud that expelled all the air from his lungs, and it took Aisling a moment to realize that a spear was sticking out of Xem's chest, extended through his torso. He looked at it for a beat before seeming to realize it was there, and then he looked up in surprise. He started to speak, but blood bubbled at his lips and ran down his chin in great dark drips.

"Xem?" The words came out of her in purest shock, even as Xemlinan slumped to his knees, eyes going dim.

"Go!" Norenn cried out, echoing down the street. He yanked her arm, hard, and she felt her legs go weak, one pulling forward with the desire to run. Before she could correct for the Red Destiny that was squeezed carefully between her thighs, it fell, hitting the loose-packed clay street with a low thud. She started to bend and pull against him to retrieve it but Norenn grabbed her elbow and yanked her onward. She caught a glimpse of guards behind them, more than two, more than a dozen, spears at the ready, and she swallowed heavily, the panic catching her.

She caught a glimpse of two of them hefting spears, ready to throw, and she ran to catch Norenn, pushing him behind the cover of the gate to their right, behind the wall she realized only belatedly was Dagonath Shrawn's estate. Two guards waited just inside, swords already drawn and within easy striking distance of both her and Norenn. One of them extended his blade and pointed it into Norenn's throat. He held it there, the silent threat implicit.

Aisling stared at them, numb shock running through her. *We were so close. So close. If we'd just been a little farther down the street ...*

There was running behind them, the sound of metal boots slapping against the road, and guards appeared at the gates, smirking. They said nothing at all, merely placed blades against her throat, hers and Norenn's, and seized them with heavy hands, dragging them back down the street to the palace they'd escaped only moments earlier.

Eleven

They took her back to the Grand Palace, locking her in a room after searching her roughly. They took her gown, her shoes, everything but her underclothes. The head guard only let her keep those after a thorough search of her person left her exposed for a few moments of terrible discomfort wherein she wondered what might come next. Finally he threw them back in her face before slamming the door and leaving her alone to put them back on, shaking as she did so.

The room was bare to the walls, carved into the cave, and had taken a long, exhausting walk to get to. Her legs were in agony and by the end, two of the guards had carried her with an arm under each elbow to speed up her pace. They took her in through a servants' entrance, Norenn dragged along behind her. They'd left Xemlinan on the street, dead, the spear still jutting from his chest.

She didn't bother to pace the room, though she might have if her legs hadn't been so weary. She sagged when she leaned against the wall, and when she sat, her buttocks grew cold and began to hurt. She stood and leaned for a few minutes, then sat, then finally lay down and stretched out on the stone floor. It was hardly the worst bed she'd had in the last few years, and was almost certain to be better than what would be coming.

She'd heard tales of the women who were sent to the Depths. They were not for the faint of heart nor weak of stomach. She tried to put that out of her mind, but thoughts of Norenn came rushing in to fill the void and she ended up alternating between the two, feeling sick over both at once.

She was in there for hours, alone, worried, thoughts about what would happen next harrying her until the iron door finally opened and a walking staff clicked the ground in front of it as a figure came in, his grey suit with waist-length coat covering his girth. She looked up and caught a glimpse of his hair, which was white and curled with age, his lined face and sunken eyes. "Do you know who I am?" he asked, without a trace of expression.

"Dagonath Shrawn," she replied and realized her mouth felt dry. It had been hours since she'd had a drop of anything to drink but her own blood.

"Quite right," he said, and with a click he brought his walking stick down again as he stepped into the room, barely sparing a look at her, even though she was nearly naked. "Do you know why you are still here?"

"No," she said, her voice much smaller than she wished it was. *Why did this have to happen?*

"Because the Sovereign wills it," Shrawn said.

"The ... Sovereign?" Aisling felt her mouth get drier.

"Oh, yes, child," Shrawn said with an amused air as he stared at the stone wall of the room. "Did you really think you could steal the Red Destiny of Saekaj?"

"Yes," she said, and her voice crackled with just a seed of defiance as she said it, but it was lost in the whisper.

"You might have gotten away with it if not for the Sovereign, if we're being truthful," Shrawn said, still looking at the wall, tearing his gaze away to finally look at her, as though he were reluctant to condescend that far. "He saw you enter the back halls from his alcove."

The Sovereign ... The words echoed in her head. *There will be no mercy ... not that there would have been, even without him.* "What happened to my friends?"

"The one with the spear through him was spared death by Amenon Lepos," Shrawn said, looking at her through half-lidded eyes. "I suppose he has a use for him, or perhaps a sentiment of some sort. It concerns him and the Sovereign now, not me." He took a step closer to her and rapped the walking stick sharply between where her feet were stretched out. "You and your lover, however, are my concern. Well, the two of you and Leneyh." He smiled a little at the mention of her name. "She'll be an enjoyable one to deal with, I think, unlike you, you bony slip of a thing."

"What happened to Norenn?" she asked, feeling the words rush out.

"I'll tell you in a moment." He almost chortled. "Do you know why I'm answering your questions? Me, of the most noble house in Saekaj, answering a lowborn thief of Sovar's questions?"

"No," she answered quickly, hoping it was the answer he was looking for. *He doesn't know who I am. He thinks I'm some street urchin.* She kept her eyes from wavering. *I must keep it that way.*

He rapped her across the mouth with the end of the walking stick, faster than she would have given the old man credit for. It stunned her, causing her to bring her hand to her mouth in shock even though it barely hurt, not even close to as much as her own punch had. The treatment she had received from the guards had been only a little rough; it was tame compared to what most would have experienced, she knew.

"Because the Sovereign willed it," Shrawn answered, turning away from her. "Because we have a growing problem, sneaking around under the corner of the horizon. It's something we have no easy answer for, nothing in place, no sure way to deal with it. It's one of a few problems. But you." He turned around and looked down at her again. "Here you are. Bold. Not stupid, but unlucky. And now completely under our power."

He crossed the distance between them and knelt down, grasping her bloodied face in his hand and pressing her head against the wall. "Most citizens of Sovar exist in this jellied state, forever within our grasp but rarely in our palm. They stay close at hand, always in easy reach but rarely in need of a firm hand. When they do," he slammed her head against the stone wall, "they find themselves in the Depths, plowing shit, tending to mushrooms, quarrying stone and mining ore." Her head ached where he'd hit it against the wall, the searing pain bringing tears to her eyes. Still, she made no sound. "We find uses for them. Angry, belligerent men have but one use—being worn down to nothing. But you …" He smiled as she opened her eyes and saw it, and it made her sick to her stomach, "you have a different use entirely."

"What do you want of me?" she asked as he pushed old, wrinkled fingers into her jawline.

"I don't want anything of you," he said, as though the very suggestion he would were something revolting to him. "Thin waif of a poor girl, I have nothing I would entrust to you and nothing I'd care to give you. But the Sovereign … he has uses for you." Shrawn withdrew his face from to hers. "Do you know the problem with a policy that calls for the death of thieves?" He sighed, not waiting for her to answer. "It makes it so hard to find exceptional liars. Certainly, there are more than a few in the nobility, but it's such a chore to convince them to do what we would have them do. No, we have more than our fair share of cruel men, of harsh and vicious ones. But ones skilled in the art of subterfuge? No weak-willed thespian will do. We need someone smart enough, clever enough … tell me girl, are you clever?" He stared down at her as though he were studying his dinner.

"Clever enough," she answered, hoping it was what he wanted to hear.

"Perhaps you are," Shrawn said, watching her, weighing her answer. "Let us see. The Sovereign wants you to understand power. Ours. Over you." He leaned in close and she smelled the remnants of the night's feast on his breath, some spices that were familiar to her from the buffet table. "Do you understand our power over you?"

"Yes," she said, whispering, as his fingers pushed against her face.

"Need I demonstrate?"

"No," she said, shaking her head quickly.

"Perhaps you are a clever girl," Shrawn said with a thin smile that disappeared a moment later. "Do you understand that if we tell you to walk along a line, you will walk that line until it falls off the edge of a cliff?" Shrawn asked, pushing her head against the wall. She could feel the pressure building in the back of her head, pain welling where he had already struck her into the stone.

"Yes," she said, and felt a tear run down her cheek, warm and salty.

"Do you understand that if you don't, we will kill your friends through methods of torture so prolonged that their own entrails will be the only meals they eat for the months that their suffering goes on?" His eyes were right in front of hers, great black orbs of hypnotic power. "Do you know that we possess healers whose sole purpose is to bring tormented souls back to life so we can torture them to death again?" He waited a moment and she nodded a fraction, as much as his fingers would allow. "And do you doubt we will visit all this and more upon your compatriots and then yourself once we find you—and find you we will, should you try to escape our grasp?"

"I believe you," she said, and the pressure lessened on the back of her head.

"What would you do to escape that fate for yourself? For your friends?" Shrawn's face started to show a gleam. "For your lover ... Norenn, is it?"

Her mouth now felt as dusty as the stone of a high cave wall. "Whatever you say." She said it, meant it, and closed her eyes, imagining Norenn. She pictured him in some room like this, beaten, flayed, and forced to relive it over and over again on Shrawn's spiteful order. *Anything to save him from that.*

"If we tell you to steal from a man, will you do it?"

"Yes," she said without hesitation.

"If we tell you to cross the world and kill a man you've never met, will you do it?"

To be an assassin of the Sovereign? She thought once more of Norenn, and her answer came easily. "Yes," she said after only a moment's pause.

"If we tell you to sleep with a man in order to learn his secrets, will you do it?"

"Yes," she answered, and this time she shook ever so slightly, pushing down the thought of betraying Norenn, pushing it down below the thought of him being tortured, tormented to death over and over. *For you, Norenn. I would do it for you, if I had to.* She blinked away a tear. *Perhaps it won't ever come to that.*

Shrawn stood, pushing his weight onto the staff and lifting himself up. He stood above her, leering down, his face lit with a smile that was filled with enormous cruelty. "Welcome to the service of the Sovereign, Aisling Nightwind." The smile grew wider. "Grow used to it, to the duty, to the quick effort of doing the Master of Saekaj and Sovar's bidding." The smile vanished as quickly as it appeared. "For you will be in the Sovereign's service until you are dead."

Twelve

Three Years Later

Aisling's skin prickled as she crossed the foyer, dead dark elves stacked in piles, waiting for morning to be dragged out. The Luukessian army was encamped within the walls, which were still fractured by the dark elves' use of Dragon's Breath powder to breach them during the siege of Sanctuary. *That was a surprise,* she conceded. *Didn't think the Sovereign would chance that.* The smell of the dead was still pungent in the air, mixed with the faint scent of the fire going in the hearth that extended along one wall.

The foyer was filled with the living as well, Luukessian refugees sleeping on blankets amidst the corpses. The doors to the Great Hall were open wide, and sleeping and huddled figures could be seen all the way to the back of that room. She ran a hand down the cloth garments she wore in place of the leather armor she'd left in her quarters earlier in the night, feeling the soft sensation of the stitched clothing; she'd gotten so accustomed to the leather armor that wearing cloth was almost like wearing nothing at all.

"Aisling," came the lilting voice of Samwen Longwell, looking weary where he stood near the far edge of the hearth. His armor was a deep navy blue, and his eyes were thinly lidded. She crossed over to him, careful to step over the figure of a child under a blanket, sleeping on the floor.

"Quite the mess around here," she said without much expression, still taking it all in.

"Yes," Longwell agreed, still wearing his full armor and leaning on his lance, the dull end of which was against the floor, reminding her most unfortunately of Dagonath Shrawn's walking stick. It always reminded her of that. "Evacuating an entire land of its surviving peoples into a place recently invaded by the dark elves has a way of being messy, I suppose."

She nodded, not wanting to be drawn into the dragoon's moodiness. "Have you seen Cyrus?"

"I have been out with a hunting party all night tracking down a dark elven general," Longwell said. "I have not seen Cyrus Davidon since the

Council meeting earlier this evening."

"Hm," Aisling said, coolly. "If he didn't go with you, he's probably still here."

"Fair assumption," Longwell said. The man looked deathly tired but still stood an exhausted vigil here. Aisling looked behind her and noted that there were others as well, Belkan and a few more, arrayed around the room, ready to repel any teleporting army.

"I'll leave you to your guard duty, then," Aisling said and slipped past him up the stairs.

"You might try his quarters," Longwell suggested, and she looked back to see him meet her gaze with a tight-lipped expression. "I doubt he's still in Council at this hour."

"Right," Aisling said, and felt her feet carry her up the steps. The jarring movement of her legs going up and down was the capstone on a day that had started with Sanctuary under siege and ended with the walls being torn down. *I need a bed. And sleep. But first, business to attend to.* It hadn't been just this day, but the accumulation of countless days, all of them. Peace was a distant memory. Comfort was something nearly forgotten, something she recalled vaguely from those days in Sovar, with Norenn at her side.

Norenn ... She put aside the thought of him. It barely brought so much as a pang of guilt anymore.

She walked down the hall of the officer quarters without a sound, easing over to the door she knew was his. She hesitated before knocking, waited a few seconds and knocked again. She heard someone moving inside before the door finally opened, and he stood before her.

"You," Cyrus said dully. She had to concede he was ruggedly handsome, even while half-asleep. His hair was long, his beard was full, and yet none of it did a thing to take away from his good looks. His muscles were visible even through the underclothes he wore in the night. And so were some of his scars.

"You sound disappointed," she said haltingly, staring at him over the threshold.

"No," he said. "Just surprised."

She stared at him, waiting for him to say something. When he didn't, she broke the silence. "May I come in?"

"Yes," he said after a moment's pause and stepped aside to let her in.

She started to pass him but as she did, he reached out for her, hand landing on her cheek as he leaned in to kiss her. She returned the kiss, leaning back into him, her fingers running over the soft fabric of his nightshirt. It was new, foreign, different from how it had been in Luukessia when she'd conquered him that first time.

He was wild, and she could feel his passion as he pressed into her. She grasped him, lifting his shirt up as she paused to get it off of him. He replied in kind and she heard the door slam shut while her cloth shirt was over her eyes. She undid his pants as they made their way to the bed, and she pushed him on it. *This was easier than I thought it was going to be.*

She slipped out of her cloth pants and was on him a moment later, lips on his until he went to her neck. She rolled to the side and let him take over, lying back as she felt a momentary chill creep up her. She encouraged him, giving him the same performance she'd given all along, since the day they'd met—every effort she made was turned toward this purpose, toward getting him to this moment.

Her hands ran along his chest. This was where she was supposed to be, after all. Where she had to be, she reflected as he entered her, his built-up lust pouring out. Exactly where they'd ordered her to be. Close enough to touch. Close enough to learn his secrets. Close enough to kill, if ever the word came to her for that.

She played the role, masking herself as she carried on doing what she'd been told. When they were finished, he fell into a deep sleep by her side. She, on the other hand, lay awake, staring at the ceiling of his quarters and pondering how little her fate—her destiny—rested in her own hands anymore.

A Note From the Author

So, a funny thing happened on the way to Thy Father's Shadow. I know, it was supposed to be the next Sanctuary release. The problem is, I got about 35,000 words into it and had to put it down. I was struggling with it, big time. I had the ending in mind, and I'd obviously written the beginning, but I was missing a critical element. Fortunately, I've figured it out, now, but I've got a few other things to write before I can get back to it. Anyway, I pushed this up in the schedule to compensate, and now at least you know who Cyrus went to bed with at the end of Crusader.

Though I'm not sure you'll be any happier with me now that you know...

Anyway, I'm working on getting the first three books in my Southern Watch series out right now, but I'm also working on Master: The Sanctuary Series, Volume Five at the same time. My hope is that by the time I get Thy Father's Shadow finished (it's a few books down the line), Master will be ready shortly thereafter. We'll see if it all goes according to plan, although if it does, it may be the first time in my writing career where that happens.

If you want to know when these books are coming, you really need to sign up for my NEW RELEASE EMAIL ALERTS. All the cool kids are doing it.

Cyrus Davidon will return in

MASTER
THE SANCTUARY SERIES
VOLUME FIVE

The disappearance and presumed death of Alaric Garaunt has thrown the guild of Sanctuary into chaos. Added to the upheaval are the sudden disappearance of Sanctuary's old allies, The Daring, the resurgence of the Dark Elves in the war, and a mystery brought to Cyrus Davidon by an old friend. As the darkness rises in the land of Arkaria, Sanctuary must find a way through their struggles to unify, even as a battle between two pillars of the guild threatens to tear them asunder once and for all.

Coming in 2014

But first...

THY FATHER'S SHADOW
A SANCTUARY NOVEL

Terian Lepos is a man without a home. Cast out of Sanctuary, he wanders the land of Arkaria until a messenger arrives with a curious offer, one that will take Terian into the darkness of Saekaj Sovar, a place he thought he had long ago left behind, and into the service of the Dark Elven Sovereignty, where he will face his worst fear – his father, and the secret that drove him from his homeland once before.

Coming in 2014!
(No, really. For real this time.)

About the Author

Robert J. Crane was born and raised on Florida's Space Coast before moving to the upper midwest in search of cooler climates and more palatable beer. He graduated from the University of Central Florida with a degree in English Creative Writing. He worked for a year as a substitute teacher and worked in the financial services field for seven years while writing in his spare time. He makes his home in the Twin Cities area of Minnesota. Now he pretty much just sits around and writes books all day long.

He can be contacted in several ways:
Via **email** at cyrusdavidon@gmail.com
Follow him on **Twitter** – @robertJcrane
Connect on **Facebook** – robertJcrane (Author)
Website – http://www.robertJcrane.com
Blog – http://robertJcrane.blogspot.com
Become a fan on **Goodreads** – http://www.goodreads.com/RobertJCrane

Other Works by Robert J. Crane

The Sanctuary Series
Epic Fantasy
Defender: The Sanctuary Series, Volume One
Avenger: The Sanctuary Series, Volume Two
Champion: The Sanctuary Series, Volume Three
Crusader: The Sanctuary Series, Volume Four
Sanctuary Tales, Volume One – A Short Story Collection
Thy Father's Shadow: A Sanctuary Novel*
Master: The Sanctuary Series, Volume Five*

The Girl in the Box
Contemporary Urban Fantasy
Alone: The Girl in the Box, Book 1
Untouched: The Girl in the Box, Book 2
Soulless: The Girl in the Box, Book 3
Family: The Girl in the Box, Book 4
Omega: The Girl in the Box, Book 5
Broken: The Girl in the Box, Book 6
Enemies: The Girl in the Box, Book 7
Legacy: The Girl in the Box, Book 8
Destiny: The Girl in the Box, Book 9*
Power: The Girl in the Box, Book 10*

Southern Watch
Contemporary Urban Fantasy
Called: Southern Watch, Book 1
Depths: Southern Watch, Book 2*

* Forthcoming

Printed in Great Britain
by Amazon